THE COMING OF DRAGONS

DARKEST AGE BOOK ONE

THE COMING OF DRAGONS

A. J. LAKE

SPECIAL THANKS TO LINDA CAREY

Published by Bloomsbury U.S.A. Children's Books
175 Fifth Avenue, New York, NY 10010
Distributed to the trade by Holtzbrinck Publishers

The Library of Congress has cataloged the hardcover edition as follows:
Lake, A. J.
The coming of dragons / by A. J. Lake. — 1st U.S. ed.
        p.   cm. — (Darkest age ; bk. 1)
Summary: Two eleven-year-olds named Edmund and Elspeth discover that they have
been given fantastic gifts to use against the ancient and evil forces that have been
awakened by powerful magic during the Dark Ages in Great Britain.
ISBN-13: 978-1-58234-965-7 • ISBN-10: 1-58234-965-7 (hardcover)
[1. Magic—Fiction. 2. Swords—Fiction. 3. Dragons—Fiction.
4. Great Britain—History—To 1066—Fiction. 5. Fantasy.]
I. Title II. Series: Lake, A. J. Darkest age ; bk. 1.
PZ7.L15849Com 2006   [Fic]—dc22   2005030623

ISBN-13: 978-1-58234-902-2 • ISBN-10: 1-58234-902-9 (paperback)

Typeset by Dorchester Typesetting Group Ltd
Printed in the U.S.A. by Quebecor World Fairfield
1 3 5 7 9 10 8 6 4 2

All papers used by Bloomsbury U.S.A. are natural, recyclable products
made from wood grown in well-managed forests. The manufacturing processes
conform to the environmental regulations of the country of origin.

For Tana Holmes Coulson - welcome

This is the Book of how Torment came.

The times were broken like a smashed lamp – tribe fighting tribe; pirates holding the North Sea to ransom, wave by wave; a new God usurping older lore. And in this brokenness, wicked seeds were sown; an ancient evil power gathered to the whisper of dark charms.

And that is how Torment came.

He began with a book of spells misused. He broke free from his frozen prison in the Far North, in the Snowlands; a glacier cracked in a burst of icy shards as his vast and scaly form roared free. Then storm and tempest filled his wings and due south he streaked, his tongue on fire, in answer to the dark-whispered call.

And as his shadow fell across the realms of Pict and Celt and Saxon, and as his huge shadow fell on the farmsteads and on the hamlets, and on the kings' halls and the slaves' huts, so men and women and children, rich men and poor shivered in their sleep and murmured: Beware, beware, beware! Torment is abroad once more.

CHAPTER ONE

Black. Then blinding white. White like split bone.

Then the wind hit. There was a sound of crashing timber like ten thousand falling trees, and the trading ship *Spearwa* stood end-up in the waves.

But it was the lightning that had done the damage. The mast was riven from top to bottom and the sail bent towards the deck like a furled swan's wing, pale in the darkness.

One of the spar's long arms sliced past Edmund's ear, missing by a hair's breadth.

'Come on!' bellowed the tillerman, yanking him off his feet, urging him on across the pitching deck. Within seconds the rain had soaked through Edmund's thin linen tunic and leggings. He gasped at the cold. But at least his boots were good. They kept him from falling as he groped through sleeting darkness, cracked his elbow on the deck house as some oarsmen pushed by, yelling to save the foremast. He saw them wrestle with fouled lines, then haul in the flapping leather sail.

For a moment Edmund saw Ship's Master Trymman standing with the rest of the rowers, yelling his commands – until the rain fell like a curtain and the master was gone, his voice drowned out in creaks and cries.

As they reached the shattered mainmast, the tillerman stopped dead and shot a look into the hammering storm. Edmund looked up too. The lightning lit a squall of hail that stung his cheeks like angry bees. He threw up a hand to shield his face, but as he did, he glimpsed something else through the flashing hail. Something that could not be there.

Fire? Surely I saw fire! He squinted up, probing the blackness between the lightning bolts. And sure enough, there it came again. A great red tongue that scorched through the dark like furnace flames.

'Gods be with us,' the tillerman mouthed, and Edmund echoed his prayer, as again the ship yawed and the waves reared up like the cliffs of Broniel.

'Hang on to the mast!' the tillerman yelled in his ear. 'Tie yourself to it!' Then he was gone, shooting across the tilting deck like a stone across ice.

But Edmund could not move. His eyes were fixed on the sky, searching the blackness for the red flashes. There! And again there. As if some gods-smith were forging fire-bolts on his anvil, the red hot sparks ripping through the sky.

He did not see the wave until it slammed his legs from under him. As the deck fell away, he slid down it, the rail flying to meet him, the boiling sea beyond. *The rail won't stop me,* he thought. *I'll be swept to my death!*

But at the last moment he grabbed hold of the spar, the one that had nearly brained him earlier. It was wedged against the rail and, still flat on his back, Edmund clung on for dear life as another wall of water sluiced over him. When he shook the sea from his eyes, he found himself staring up at a face. A girl's face, with eyes of fierce amber.

'Use this!' the girl cried, throwing him a rope. 'Or you'll rip your arms off.' The rope's other end was wound fast round the mast stump. Edmund hauled himself up towards it, binding the rope tightly round his hands.

He saw the girl had already tethered herself to the mast, made a cat's cradle of ropes round waist and chest to ride out the storm. Her calmness astonished him.

'You're the shipmaster's daughter,' he shouted above the wind, his teeth clattering as he shivered from cold and wet and fear that tasted like steel against his tongue.

'Elspeth Trymmansdaughter,' she yelled back. 'And you're the passenger. The one who never leaves his cabin.'

'I'm here now,' he muttered.

'Not for long,' the girl said flatly.

And then Edmund realised it wasn't only he who was shuddering. The *Spearwa* herself was shaking from stem to stern, the timbers screaming beneath his feet.

Eyes half-closed to the lashing spray, Edmund clung to the wet rope, cursing himself for a coward. He was a king's son, heir to Heored of Sussex, and here he was shivering like a whipped dog when he should be facing death with a man's resolve. It was what his mother would expect. He tried to straighten himself and meet the girl's stare, but suddenly all he could see was his mother's face: her dark eyes and brown hair. Her kind looks. He saw her brave smile as they had parted at the Noviomagus quayside two days before.

She had been so worried for his safety on this voyage. When she had discovered that the ship's master was a follower of the new Christian faith, she had spent an hour at their household shrine, sacrificing to the Lady Donn and to her namesake goddess, Branwen, begging them to bless Edmund's journey. She had chosen this packet-boat because it took the long route, hugging the coast to avoid the pirate Danes who prowled the eastern seas. Only once they reached Dunmonia, the Isles' most westerly realm, would the boat take to the open sea and cross the Channel.

'Avoid questions,' his mother had commanded with a last fierce hug. 'Stay out of sight, and talk to no one but the ship-master. If you must speak, say your father is a merchant fallen on hard times. That he went to Gaul to sell his cloth and has sent word for you to join him.'

As Edmund had listened to his mother's instruction, his eyes had pricked with tears. He'd blinked them away, of course. At eleven years old he was almost a man and to cry was shameful. He'd drawn himself up to his full height, as if to give his mother no quarter.

'Can I ask *you* a question?' he had demanded. 'Why aren't you coming with me?'

As soon as he had spoken he wished he hadn't. He saw the pain dart in her eyes. But when she spoke it was in the level tones of a wise queen, not an indulgent mother.

'You know that very well, Edmund. Your father may never return, and when this madness is over someone must take up his burden. Who would that be, if this ship went down with both you and me on board?'

And now the Lady Donn and the goddess Branwen had deserted him, leaving his mother alone in Noviomagus. Edmund wondered how long it would take for news of the shipwreck to reach his father's kingdom fifty leagues away. He thought of the homeland he would never again see – the rolling downlands and fair pastures and good farms – and his throat tightened till he could hardly breathe.

A shriek of tortured wood shocked him to his senses. Something scraped against the keel and again the ship shook from end to end. He heard the shipmaster bellow an order, saw the girl suddenly straining in her rope web. This time he saw fear in the amber eyes.

She was shouting at him, but the wind whipped her words away. He caught only 'rocks!' and 'Manacles!'.

It was enough. Even a landsman like Edmund knew of the Manacles, the merciless basalt fangs that reared from the sea south of Stannan Head. Scarcely a moon passed without some unwary ship ripping her keel out on them. Edmund peered across the water and saw only darkness, blotched with foam. But soon the oarsmen's frantic yells were echoing Elspeth's words – *ROCKS! MAN-A-CLES! LOOK OU-UT!* – and the crewmen fought to turn the sail on the only surviving mast.

'What can we do?' Edmund cried.

'Tell your gods your sins,' replied the girl.

Edmund glanced round with mounting panic. Sailors slid all over the deck as the giant waves rolled over the salt-stained planks. In horror Edmund watched an oarsman dashed against the rail, then tossed in the sea. As the deck dipped further, he glimpsed a white hand raised in brief appeal; then nothing but the reeling waves. The other rowers barely spared their shipmate a glance, but bent to their oars as if all the fiends of hell were at their backs. *They know*, Edmund thought. *They know all is lost.*

He turned to Elspeth, but her eyes were closed. Perhaps she was praying. He thought of his mother's gods and wracked his brains: had he offended the sea god Llyr, or Manawydan lord of winds? Again his eyes flew to the sky . . .

By all the gods! As if walls of sea weren't bad enough! Now the world was spinning on its head like some frenzied top.

On its head!

Instead of looking up, he was looking *down, down* at the sea that pitched all around him. *Down* into the blackness where he was being tossed. And from this new sky-view he could see the *Spearwa*, its timbers straining. He could see tiny creatures, spindly two-legged things, scattered on the deck. Waves swatting them back and forth like a man swats flies. Soon, he thought, soon all would be gone, the planks blown apart; the sea empty once more.

Only one tiny soul looked up at him, its face a white disc topped with pale hair. Its eyes wide; its mouth a dark O, and opened in a scream that filled his head . . .

Edmund was watching himself. He was seeing himself clinging to the mast rope. And the screaming would not stop. And then his eyes came back to him and he squeezed the lids shut to stop their eerie looking. He shut his mouth too, silenced the scream, and then, dizzy and trembling, clung like a barnacle to the sea-drenched ropes.

A slap of spray brought him to his senses. He blinked salt out of his eyes. He was back on deck with the storm raging around him, men battling frantically at their oars. Nearby, the girl was watching him with a strange look in her eyes. What had she seen? Before he could ask her, the ship grounded with an ear-splitting crash; the deck blew apart, sending Edmund spinning.

This time there was no spar to save him. On his back, half-stunned, the next wave caught him as it swept down the breaking deck. But just for an instant, before the sea took him, Edmund glimpsed the sky and saw it.

A great, winged shape hovered above them, larger than

the ship itself. It gleamed an unnatural blue in every flash of lightning. An eye the size of a warrior's shield looked down with cold purpose on Edmund. And the mouth, a fiery cave with stalagmite teeth, grinned wider as the ship broke in two.

CHAPTER TWO

As the waves reared like walls, Elspeth felt her faith slip away. *Lord, what have you done?* How could the sea she loved so well become her deadly foe? She shut her eyes tight and braced herself in her mesh of ropes as the *Spearwa* plunged beneath the waves. Down through the drowning swell they pitched, till she thought they would never right themselves again.

Never had she seen such a storm, not in all her life at Dubris port, as well known for its roaring winter seas as for its towering white cliffs, from which you could see Gaul on a clear day. She had not seen a storm like this in all the three years she had been sailing with her father, and they had endured their share of gales off Penseance many times over.

But this storm was different. It had blown up from nowhere – out of a calm spring night.

Now with every crack of timber, cold terror gripped her. Not that she would let that pale, scared boy see her fear. She was a seafarer, and proud to ply a trade more usually the domain of men. The sea was her life, her love, since her mother had died of fever and her father had brought her aboard. Some of the crew had muttered darkly, of course; there had been some hard looks at first, but she had won them over. She'd learned fast, reading the compass, helping her father check the goods in the hold against the tally sticks, even reefing the sails with Master Seaman Harkiron. And now, at eleven years old, it was well known that one day Elspeth Trymmansdaughter would succeed her father and become master of the *Spearwa*.

But now all seemed to be lost, and Elspeth thought fearfully of her father, still battling with the tiller, and longed to be at his side in this war with the sea.

When the pale boy screamed her eyes snapped open. Ahead a black spur reared up like the tower of the godshouse at Bradwell, with more columns of basalt behind like black dragon's teeth. But the boy stared only at the sky. What had made him cry out like that?

Crash!

The *Spearwa* slewed into the massive pillar of rock. Elspeth clung tight to her harness. But the boy had nothing to hold him fast. When the deck reared up, he went sprawling backwards to the starboard rail. In a moment he was gone, swallowed by the sea.

Screams and curses rang in Elspeth's ears, but then they too were drowned. Next came more terrible crunching of splitting wood. *Father!* But her scream blew away with the spray, into the dark where only chaos ruled. She saw one of the sailors – Bron, she thought – pitch past her. As he fought for a footing on the deck it seemed he was dancing. The next moment he hit the rail smack in the ribs and folded forward into the sea.

Now the boards beneath Elspeth's feet began to crack like kindling. She gasped as the ropes clutched like a snake. If she didn't loose the knots, the tumbling mast stump would drag her through the hold and snap her back like a twig.

But the knots were slick and swollen with water, and Elspeth's hands were stiff with cold.

She fumbled for the scaling-knife at her belt; prayed to her father's stern-faced god that it still had an edge from the last time she'd stropped it. All fingers and thumbs, she sawed at the first rope, and then at another, while around her the *Spearwa* gave up its struggle against the rocks and sank, piece by piece, into the frothing sea.

She felt the mast list towards her, the planks sagging beneath it. Now! Now she must move. She struggled out of the remaining ropes. But one foot was caught. It twisted painfully as the mast leaned closer still. She tugged, and tugged again, and dragged it free as the mast crashed through the planks where she had just been kneeling.

Elspeth turned to stern: that was where her father would be. But before she had gone two steps, the remaining deck planks parted under her feet and she fell in a storm of rent wood.

Down and down she plunged.

For an age Elspeth floundered. Strong swimmer she may have been, but the sea's cold stunned her – and made her desperate to cling to this life. After all, her father might not be dead. She forced herself to think, to move. *Which way is up?* her mind screamed. At last she kicked her legs, arched her back and, finding gravity's pull, pushed through the churning swell towards the surface. On and up she fought, and just when she thought her lungs would burst, she breached the waves and gulped down ragged shards of air.

But again the waves took her down, tossing her round and round like a rag doll in a mill race. She let it take her. To fight now would use up precious energy. And so three times more she rose and fell, gulping a mouthful of air whenever she could. On the third time a great bolt of lightning lit up the rocks below her and the basalt spires of a seabed city reared up through the hissing waves. In desperation, Elspeth twisted away, struggling with every breath in her body.

Gasping, she broke the surface, into the frenzy of rain and hail. She cast about for sign of the *Spearwa*, but what with the night and the stinging spray she could scarcely see two yards ahead. No men. No wreckage.

'Father!' she screamed. 'Father, where are you?' But the crashing of sea on stone drowned out her cry.

She felt the fight drain out of her then. What was the point? She was tiring fast. She could not win this battle with the waves. But just when she thought to give up, the storm threw her an unexpected gift. A wooden chest broke the surface close by. With a burst of new strength, she struck out for it and caught hold of one of its handles. It was oak chased in iron, sturdy and strong and seemingly proof against the waves. Elspeth clung to it, gasping and gathering her strength.

The next thing she saw was a body. She almost let go of the chest with the shock of it. Like all Dubris children she knew what the sea did to the dead. Scenes of white, bloated faces, seaweed-twined limbs flooded her mind. But she forced herself to look for it again among the tossing waves. It might have been any one of the *Spearwa*'s crew: Beron or Inch. It could have been her own father! *He could still be alive!*

She searched about her for the wave-born figure. Then she saw it, a dark, limp form in the jagged sea. This time she struck out towards it, leaving behind the sea-chest haven.

The waves dragged her crazily to right and left, threw her like a ball, and the rain and spray merged in a world of snarling water.

When she saw the body again it was a few yards to her right. Clawing her way through the heavy swell, she snatched a sleeve and hauled it to her. It was lighter than she had expected, and moved easily. And then she saw why: it was not a seaman, but the boy, Edmund. Alive or dead she could not tell – but dead for sure if she couldn't get him back to the sea chest.

She looked for it again in the darkness, knowing her own death was certain if she didn't find it. Beside her the boy dipped beneath the waves, and again she hauled him to the surface. And just when she thought all was lost, there was a hideous flare of red light and in its glow she saw the chest was no more than five yards away. She hooked one hand around the boy's neck, and struggled clumsily towards it. *Please*, she thought. *Please let us reach the chest . . .*

The sky bled fire like a bullock with its throat cut. Aagard bared his teeth in the dark and mouthed a silent curse. From turbid East to drowning West, men would be staring in horror into that blood-boltered sky. Aagard winced as he saw more bursts of fire across the sea. A great evil had been loosed in this night's storm, with worse to come.

The old man turned from the sea with a sinking heart. There was nothing he could do about the storm, and at this moment he had more pressing business. Life and death business, if he was not mistaken. He trudged along the rain-drenched beach, counting his steps in the face of the storm.

Ninety-three. Ninety-four. Ninety-five.

He stopped and looked out beyond the waves. This was where the dream had told him to come, but it had not told him what he would find. Only that something would come out of the storm, something of great importance that must be kept safe at all costs; something that might not look outwardly precious . . .

Aagard frowned as another fiery tongue seared the sky. *Outwardly precious!* As if he needed his dreams to warn him about outward trappings! He had learned that grim lesson two years ago in Venta. These days it was only his soul, his dreams, his mind's eye that he trusted; even so, he thought wryly, this particular dream might have been a little more specific . . .

At last he saw it. Something bobbing in the tide's white horses. A black shape looming in the storm's reflecting glow. It was too far out to reach, first drifting in towards the strand and then clawed back in the undertow.

Quite suddenly, with the ninth wave there it was, deposited directly before him, ten strides out on the wet sands. Aagard stared at it, half expecting some further revelation to explain its purpose and his mission. And that was when he realised: it was not one thing, but three.

Aagard picked his moment carefully. He was too old to fight the sea, but he couldn't risk losing this strange delivery. Yet as he paused, some inner voice nagged: *Trust your dream! Watch the sky! Act now, before it is too late!* He struggled across the sucking sands to the largest of the three shapes. It turned out to be a sturdy oak chest.

A stillness came over him. The chest was familiar; ominously familiar. He had hoped never to see it again. And to see it now of all times, on this night of unnatural storm, made his blood run cold. Uncertain and fearful, he knelt to look at the padlock. It was still firm, the runes around it blackened with age and wear, but seemingly untouched.

'Well, then,' he muttered. 'We're not wholly undone. Not yet.'

He leant over the chest to see what else the sea had brought him, and gasped.

Of all the things he had thought might come to him out of the madness and malice of the storm, this was the least likely, and the most baffling. But no, he had seen them before! This dark girl and pale, pale boy. Now he remembered. Had he not also glimpsed them in the dream?

The children of the storm.

CHAPTER THREE

Edmund rose, gulping, from the waves. Above him the huge winged monster swept down . . . his breath turned to stone . . . he lashed out . . .

Edmund's eyes flicked open in disbelief. Instead of the storm's roar there was quietness, and instead of freezing wetness there was warmth, and the burst of red that had so terrified him before was only firelight crackling in a hearth. The scaly apparition had disappeared. The storm was gone. He was safe.

Gods be praised. His mother's offerings for a safe journey had worked after all. Edmund gazed around him. He was in some kind of cave. Candles flickered on high stony ledges, casting little pools of light. Beneath him was the rustle of clean straw over which a warm blanket had been spread. Even his clothes were almost dry – steaming a little in the heat from the fire. Next to him the girl slept on, under a blanket of her own. Edmund stared at her sun-bronzed cheek, where black strands of hair stirred a little on her breath. That dark hair made him think of his mother again, and again the storm came roaring back. His heart leapt with shock. The last thing he had seen was . . . was that thing in the sky . . . then the waves burying him. What had happened? How had they got here? And *where* were they?

The cave was furnished like a learned man's chamber, with a shelf of books against one wall and a lectern on which to rest the larger volumes so as to read them more easily. There was also a table and stools, and on the table a platter and knife set out for a meal.

Beyond the firelight, someone was speaking very quietly. No. It was singing rather than speaking; a man's low voice, chanting words he could not fathom. Edmund raised himself on his elbow, wincing at the stiffness in his arms.

In the furthest corner of the cave a man was standing with his back to him. He was bending over something with his hands outstretched, and as Edmund watched he finished his chanting and knelt down. There was a small, metallic noise; then the man straightened up, sighing. But he seemed to know Edmund was awake for he turned calmly and came over to him.

He was old, his face seamed and wrinkled and his beard more silver than black. But his eyes held a piercing and unsettling darkness, and his carriage was proud. He stood like a king, or a man used to speaking with kings.

'You are welcome here,' the man said. His voice was clipped, but not unkind, and his accent more like Edmund's than he might have expected so far to the west.

The old man raised his eyebrows in faint enquiry, and Edmund said, 'My name is Edmund.' He was not prepared to give away any more of his identity than this, especially as he knew nothing about this man. Was he rescuer, or captor?

Suddenly the man bent closer and searched Edmund's face as if trying to solve a riddle. 'You are wondering where you are,' he said. 'This place is called Gullsedge, and you are in my home.'

'How did I get here?' Edmund asked. His voice sounded strange – low and hoarse. 'I was . . . a wave swept me off the deck, while I was looking at . . .' He hesitated. How could he describe the thing that he had seen in the eye of the storm? No one sane would believe him. He glanced across at the girl. She was still asleep, oblivious. Had she seen it too?

'I am Aagard,' said the old man. 'Once of the kingdom of Wessex, now of Dunmonia. The sea cast you up here; you and something else.' Once again, he gave Edmund a searching look. 'If you are well enough to stand, there's something I would like to show you.'

He turned and walked away, further into the cave, and Edmund rose shakily to his feet and followed, shivering at the night's dank air beyond the firelight.

Aagard went to the thing he had been bending over before. It was a chest, rimed with salt water and draped with bladder-wrack. It looked very old and its metal edges were black and corroded. A huge padlock of rusted iron held it shut, but as far as Edmund could see, the lock had no keyhole.

Aagard pointed at the chest. 'What is this?' he asked. 'And where did it come from?'

Edmund stared at him, confused. 'I don't know. I've never seen it before.'

'It was washed up alongside you,' Aagard said. 'Did you not cling to it when your ship broke up?'

Edmund shook his head. He had no recollection of anything after the waters closed over his head.

The old man looked again at the chest. 'But it must have come from the ship on which you travelled,' he persisted. 'Do you really not know where –'

'Wareham,' said a new voice.

Edmund and Aagard turned to see Elspeth walking stiffly towards them. 'We took it aboard at Wareham. My father loaded it himself.' She broke off and curtsied awkwardly. 'Elspeth Trymmansdaughter, sir,' she said. 'Is it you I must thank for my life?'

Aagard waved her words away. 'You came alive out of the flood, so it is your own strength and spirit that should be thanked.'

'Even so,' Elspeth insisted, 'you brought us here, and gave us shelter.' Before Aagard could speak she went on, 'But can you tell me, sir – was there anyone else? Any other men from the ship, or wreckage, even? My father . . .' Her voice trailed off as she read the answer in Aagard's face.

'There were only the two of you,' he said. 'But the village of Medwel is only a league away down the coast path. Ships wrecked on the rocks often wash up there, and survivors too sometimes. Have no fear, the villagers will care for any that they find. Tomorrow you can go there and enquire.'

Elspeth nodded unhappily and Edmund felt a stab of sympathy for her. She turned her head to hide her tears, and Edmund looked away too.

'But first,' Aagard went on, 'there are things I must ask you.' He indicated the chest. 'I have seen this before, and I fear its coming here bodes no good. Did you see who brought it to your ship?'

'It was an old man,' Elspeth said. 'He wore a red gown – like that one.' She pointed to a long robe, wine-red in colour, that hung from an iron hook on the wall.

Edmund frowned. The tunic Aagard was wearing was grey wool, patched and thin-looking, but the robe that hung from the hook was altogether richer. A lord might have worn it, or a companion to a king. He looked at his host with a new interest.

'The man who brought the chest gave my father some trouble,' Elspeth went on, smiling at the memory. 'He insisted on going aboard to see it stowed for safe delivery to Gaul. He said there would be someone to meet it when we reached the harbour. Father said he was so careful of the old box, he'd wager there were jewels in it.'

'Thrimgar,' Aagard muttered. 'He would not have sent it away except in the direst need . . .' He stopped and looked at Elspeth more gently. 'You are tired, child. Rest by the fire. I'll bring you food shortly, when I have spoken with your companion.'

'He's not –' Elspeth began, but then she shrugged and went over to the fire, stretching her palms out to catch its warmth.

Edmund opened his mouth to say he knew nothing that could be of use; that he had barely been on deck during the voyage, and had no memory of seeing the chest before now. But Aagard bade him sit down at the table, fixing him once more with that piercing gaze.

'You have not told me everything, have you?' the old man pressed quietly. 'Believe me, I know this night's storm was no common one. If you saw something there, let me know of it.'

Edmund felt his face grow hot. 'Did *you* . . . ?' he began. But he didn't even know how to ask the question: did you see something flying through the sky tonight, something that has no business outside old wives' tales and children's stories?

'Did I see the dragon?' Aagard finished for him.

Edmund stared across the table, speechless.

The old man went on, 'No, my boy, I did not see him, but in my dream I felt the evil that could conjure him. Such a creature has not been seen in many generations, and his coming now bodes great evil. The storm was only the start.'

Edmund shuddered, remembering the vast beast hovering over the stricken ship; the monstrous eye rolling above him as he lay on the splitting deck. Only for a moment had he stared into that eye, but its cruel gaze had burned into his mind like a brand.

'His name is Torment,' said Aagard. 'You need feel no shame if you were afraid. Strong men have wept to face him. Gods have died fighting him.'

Edmund did not answer.

The old man gave him a wintry smile. 'You thought dragons were a fable? It's true that they have been kept apart from men for centuries. But they can return, with reason enough. What you saw was real, I promise you.'

'There's something else,' Edmund blurted out. Before he could think better of it, he told Aagard of the dizzying moments before the wreck, when he seemed to leave the *Spearwa* and hover high above the ship, looking down at his own body. 'I thought I was running mad,' he confessed.

Aagard eyed him gravely, with no trace of contempt or even surprise. 'It was no fantasy,' he said. 'You are – let me see – eleven years old?' Edmund nodded, wondering where this was leading. 'And on the ship, when you looked down at yourself,' the old man continued, 'were you still afraid of the storm?'

'Of course I . . .' Edmund stopped. For those few dizzying moments, he had not been afraid at all. He had looked down at the ship as if it were a piece of wood swarming with insects. He had *rejoiced* to see it swept away! Edmund bowed his head in horror and confusion.

Aagard touched him softly on the arm. 'You were not losing your mind,' he said. 'You were looking through another's eyes. The dragon's.'

I was what? Edmund searched the man's face, too shocked to speak. What was he saying?

'Tell me, what do you know of the Ripente?'

Edmund flinched as if Aagard had struck him. Every great household had heard of the Ripente: a rare line of second-sighted men and women, who could look into a man's mind and out through his eyes, seeing as he saw. They were outsiders wherever they went, treated as a race apart and used as spies and informers by anyone who could pay them well enough.

Aagard looked at him with narrowed eyes. 'You know something, I can see that. It would be unusual for you to be the first in the family. Does your father have these powers also?'

Edmund flared with indignation. 'The Ripente are nothing but treacherous vagabonds! Men with no lords, without loyalty to anyone. My father . . .' He stopped, recalling his mother's warning just in time. He must not give away his father's name. 'My family is an honourable one,' he finished stiffly. 'No spies or traitors ever shared our blood.'

'And yet you have the Ripente power,' Aagard said mildly.

'No!' Edmund was furious now. 'If a . . . a *dragon* takes hold of my mind . . .'

'He did no such thing,' Aagard broke in, a new edge to his voice. '*You* took hold of *his* mind. And he could not have known it, or he would have killed you.'

Edmund fell silent. Aagard took him by the shoulders and

looked into his face. 'I have some knowledge of the Ripente,' he said. 'I suspected when you first opened your eyes that you might possess the skill. But to look through the eyes of a dragon . . .' He dropped his hands, and his voice became urgent.

'You have a great power. That does not make you a spy, or a traitor. Yes, the Ripente have often been outcasts. People always fear what they cannot understand. And it's true that some Ripente have used their skills selfishly, for gain and power. But *you* need not!'

Sitting by the fire, Elspeth heard their voices raised, as if in argument. Edmund was so haughty, she thought: could he not even bring himself to be polite to the man who had taken them in? But she did not greatly care. Her mind was filled with her father as she had seen him last, calling orders as he hauled the tiller round, calm and purposeful in the face of the storm that would split his boat into kindling. *I won't cry,* she told herself fiercely. *Even if he's drowned, he would have wanted no other death. But he's* not *dead; he's a stronger swimmer than I am. I won't believe that he's dead.*

Unable to sit still any longer, Elspeth climbed stiffly to her feet and began to wander around the cave, running her hand over the rough stone walls. Ahead of her was the chest that had saved their lives, the salt-rimed piece of flotsam that had brought them to this place. It looked older than anything she had ever seen; even older than the saints' reliquaries in the great godshouse at Durovernum. But more intriguing still was the lock. How was it meant to be opened with no keyhole? Elspeth knelt down and ran her hand over the blind, seamless face of the padlock.

There was a grinding rasp of metal against metal and the hasp of the lock sprang free.

In surprise, she turned to call to Aagard, but he was leaning towards the boy, speaking so earnestly that she did not like to interrupt. She turned back to the chest. Slowly, she slid the lock out of the wards and pulled them up. The lid swung open soundlessly, as though its hinges had just been oiled instead of soaked with sea. The chest exhaled a sour whiff of ancient air.

Inside, it was dark unvarnished wood, giving back no reflection from the candlelight. At first Elspeth thought it was empty, but something glimmered at the bottom. She bent in for a closer look and the thing grew brighter, as if a pale flame suddenly shone within it.

It was a gauntlet made of finely wrought silver facets, each one overlapping its neighbour so they rippled like the scales of some magical fish. Elspeth's eyes widened. Surely no silver mined from the earth could have that living shimmer? Or perhaps some minuscule creatures from the sea's depths, those that shine with their own light, had attached themselves to the surface of the gauntlet as the waves turned it over and over. And yet that couldn't be, for the inside of the chest was bone dry.

Entranced, she reached down to touch it.

The cry that rang round the cave froze Edmund's blood. He flung up his arms like a shield as a white light blinded him.

But in a moment it was gone. When the light's dazzle had cleared, Edmund saw Aagard staring open-mouthed across the cave.

Elspeth stood before them, her right arm held straight out as if it were stone. On her hand was a shimmering, silver gauntlet – and in her grasp was a sword of pure, translucent crystal.

CHAPTER FOUR

Elspeth was rigid with shock. The sword, shining with its own light and longer than her arm, filled her sight so that she could not look away. She tried to open her hand and drop it, but her fingers would not unbend inside the gauntlet. One cold winter she had taken hold of an icicle. The silver glove burned and clung to her skin in just the same way. She tried to throw the sword from her, but there was such a stab of agony that she screamed.

'Help me! Take it off!'

Dimly, she saw Edmund jump to his feet, knocking over his stool. Aagard was already on his feet; he crossed swiftly to her side, but did not touch her and, as Edmund ran up, he held the boy back.

'The pain will fade soon,' he said. Even through her terror, and the burning needles stabbing her body, Elspeth could see that the old man's face was white. She bit down another scream, breathing in great gasps, and held herself stiffly, feeling that the slightest move or touch would only make the pain worse.

Just as Elspeth thought her knees would buckle with exhaustion, the pain began to ebb. When the burning died down to a dull throb, she let her arm fall. The sword hung by her side, glowing with a cold fire. *What is this?* Elspeth thought in terror.

Aagard took her by the shoulders and led her back to her seat at the hearth. Elspeth scarcely noticed the warmth of the flames. When she didn't stop shivering, Aagard fetched the red robe from its hook on the wall and draped it around her shoulders. The sword-shaped light shone out against the rich material, pulsing to an unheard rhythm.

'The lock opened itself,' Elspeth whispered, between chattering teeth. 'I only touched the glove, and then it was on my hand. I never meant to –'

Aagard silenced her with a gesture. 'What you meant and what *it* meant,' he murmured, 'are worlds apart.'

His words made no sense to Elspeth. 'I can't put it down!' she cried. 'It sticks to my hand, look! Can you not take it from me?'

Aagard took a step backwards, spreading his hands in denial or helplessness.

Elspeth pleaded with him, 'But I can't –'

She heard the boy cry out, 'Look! It's changing!'

Elspeth glanced down. The sword's glow had begun to fade. As she watched, both sword and gauntlet became insubstantial, the blade thinning to the faintest edge in the air. A moment later there was only a shimmering haze around her hand and arm. But she could still feel the echo of its weight, and the lingering press of the hilt in her gloved hand.

'It's gone,' said Edmund.

'No,' said Aagard. 'It has returned. It will not leave till its work is done.'

Elspeth stared at him. The pressure in her hand was easing. She flexed her fingers and rubbed at her palm, glad to feel skin and sinew, not jointed steel.

'What do you mean?' she demanded. 'Will this happen again?'

There was concern in Aagard's face as he looked at her, but something else as well – a spark of excitement.

'It cannot be chance,' he murmured. His gaze flickered from her to Edmund, and he seemed to come to a decision. 'Come sit with me, both of you. There are matters we must discuss.'

'I have never seen the sword before,' Aagard told them when they were seated by the fire, drinking soup from wooden bowls, 'but it was in my care for eighteen years, when I served in the King's Rede of Venta Bulgarum.'

Edmund felt a stirring of curiosity. The red cloak made sense now.

'The King's Rede?' he echoed. 'You were a king's counsellor?'

'I was liegeman to Beotrich, King of Wessex.' The old man's face was sombre. 'My lord the king still lives, but the Rede – his council of trusted advisors – has been disbanded.'

He sighed. 'There were seven of us: thanes and scholars every one. One of our responsibilities was guarding the royal treasures, chief among them the crystal sword.

'The chest that held the sword had been passed down through generations, sealed and protected by sorcery. No one in living memory has been able to open it.' He glanced at Elspeth, but she avoided his eyes, staring down at her bowl of soup. She was using her hand normally, although from time to time Edmund saw her stroke the bowl as if seeking comfort from the rough wood beneath her fingertips.

'But everyone knew the legends and the prophecy,' Aagard continued. 'The crystal sword was once used to rid the kingdom of a great evil. If the realm was ever in desperate need, it was said that the chest would open, the sword would reappear – and a new hero would rise to bear it.'

Elspeth looked up sharply. 'Then why did it come to me? I don't want it!'

'Maybe in part *because* you do not want it,' Aagard replied softly. 'No one who tried to open the chest has ever succeeded. I tried myself, just before the two of you woke up. I know as much of the runes that bound the lock as any man living. Yet I failed.' He looked from Elspeth to Edmund.

'The last person who *wanted* the crystal sword has ruined an entire kingdom with the strength of his twisted desire. His name is Orgrim, and I knew him when I was in Venta Bulgarum. He was the youngest of the King's Rede, and yet the most valued by King Beotrich.' Aagard's face clouded. 'Orgrim was not a Wessex man like the rest of us. He came to Venta in an exchange of hostages five years ago. Such were his talents, and so great his devotion to our king, that we all agreed to admit him to the Rede.

'Orgrim soon began to show interest in the prophecies of the crystal sword. He asked the other Redesmen about it, but we knew little more than the stories themselves. So he began to read, hoping to find the knowledge he sought in voices even older than ours. He borrowed books of ancient lore from us and devoured them with tireless eyes. Only one book we held back. Our leader, Thrimgar, had a volume of necromancy, which he felt was too dangerous to show to anyone.'

Elspeth looked blankly at Aagard.

'A book of spells,' Edmund whispered to her.

'Like weather charms?' Elspeth was still puzzled.

'It was the spellbook of an old and powerful sorcerer,' Aagard explained. 'Such magics have the power to do great evil as well as good. Foremost among them was the power to summon dragons . . . One day this book went missing.'

Now the old man's face was dark; his voice low with remembered anger. 'Thrimgar and I found Orgrim kneeling by the chest, the book of spells open beside him. He had filled the room with smoke, and there was blood on the lock of the chest. He said not a word when he saw us, but ran from the room. We summoned the council that day and agreed to ask

King Beotrich to expel Orgrim from the Rede, for betrayal of his trust and the use of black magic. But when we came to the king, Orgrim had already dripped poison in his ear.'

Aagard's voice shook. 'King Beotrich accused us of treason. He said that Orgrim had uncovered a plot among us to overthrow him, that the Rede was dissolved, and that we were under arrest. Orgrim held the king in his thrall so completely, he would not listen to anything we had to say. He ordered soldiers to lead us away, but they were good honest men and knew the accusation was false. One of them allowed Thrimgar and me to escape; I never heard what happened to the other four.'

'And the chest?' Elspeth prompted.

'We dared not leave it there! We carried it with us when we fled, and swore to guard it till death. I wanted to bring it here, but Thrimgar insisted that the sword was sacred to Wessex and had to remain in the kingdom. When I left, two years ago, Thrimgar went into hiding with the chest at Wareham. But now, after all, he has sent it away. Which means some danger must have come that was beyond his powers to protect the sword. If Orgrim still has the book of spells, he can summon evil far beyond the compass of our good magic.'

'I don't understand,' Edmund said. 'What does Orgrim mean to do with the crystal sword, if not to use it to defend Wessex and his king?'

'I do not know precisely,' Aagard said. 'And I will not try to guess. Some evils are best not spoken of before they appear.'

'But,' Edmund persisted, 'why would Beotrich take this man's word over yours? You had all been the king's men from birth. You said Orgrim was an outsider, some foreign hostage?'

Aagard stared into the fire. 'It is one of life's bitterest lessons,' he sighed. 'And one that you will both learn before all this is finished. Evil comes in many guises, and when it puts on charming ways and handsome looks and clear-eyed youthful wisdom, it is the most treacherous of all.' He turned to them, a deep sadness in his eyes. 'We all admired Orgrim. Every one of us. He was brave as well as wise beyond his years. But there was more than that. Orgrim had a skill that no other in the Rede possessed, and that made him the most valued advisor of all. When he told the king that he had uncovered a plot, he did not need to say that he had heard rumours, or found evidence. He said that he *knew*. That he had looked through our eyes and felt our treachery.'

Edmund shivered. He wanted to hear no more of this story.

Aagard's gaze burned into him as he said, 'Orgrim was a Ripente.'

Edmund lay on the straw pallet, watching the firelight flicker on the roof of the cave. A few feet away, he could hear Elspeth restlessly curling and uncurling. He felt sorry for her, and curious too: the gods had marked out a cruel destiny for her, to have lost her father and now to suffer this new pain, as real as knife wounds from the way she had looked when the light shone from her hand. But how could a sword appear and then vanish? And if Aagard was right, why would this fabled weapon attach itself to an unskilled girl?

Suddenly Edmund's own misery overwhelmed him. Why was he worrying about this girl he hardly knew, when his troubles were just as bad?

He could *not* be a Ripente; it was unthinkable. Aagard's story about Orgrim had made it clear what they were: a race of vipers, of traitors. To be a Ripente was to be without loyalty: who had told him that, Edmund wondered? Not his father. He could not remember either of his parents ever mentioning the subject to him. Loyalty and duty were the watchwords of their lives. How could their child be one of the faithless ones?

Edmund shut his eyes tightly, longing for mindless sleep.

He dozed unhappily, and found himself in a strange place. A dream but not a dream. He was standing on a pebbly slope beneath a wide, cloud-filled sky. There were tussocks of brittle sea holly. Behind was the sound of the surf, more gentle now as it rose and fell on the shingle where small boats had been hauled up. A gull shrieked above him, and ahead, up the slope, someone was chopping wood.

Edmund followed the sound. Over the hill's brow he saw the walls of a small settlement, a dozen thatched houses around a rough green with fish-drying huts and workshops. A dog barked and the smoke of cooking-fires drifted from the

45

roof-holes. Someone was grinding grain, by the sound of it. It could be a fishing village in Edmund's own kingdom.

As he drew closer, an unaccountable fear gripped him. He found himself running in terror towards the first house, knowing something dreadful was about to happen. Before he reached it, a sheet of fire roared up the thatch. Smoke billowed round him in black choking gusts and the straw spat and crackled, showering him with sparks.

Suddenly there were people everywhere, fleeing in mindless panic with their beasts – a pig, some scorched hens, women screaming, babes howling, angry man-shouts. Edmund stumbled over a bleeding child, then collided with a shrieking man, his hair alight. He saw the fire whip up a fishing net hung out to dry. Then all was lost in the smoke and Edmund fell to his knees on the open ground between the drying huts.

There was nothing he could do to help these people. Three more homes were already blazing up like sacrificial pyres.

Viking fiends! Edmund cursed. He cast round for a weapon, surprised that the yellow-haired hordes had reached this far west. There had been fewer attacks on his kingdom this winter, and he and his mother had thought the invaders had been distracted by raids to the far north-east.

And then Edmund saw them.

They were not straw-haired Danes. These men were mounted, two dozen riders clad not in mail, but in tunics and breeches of fine, dark cloth. On their heads, tight domed helmets gleamed like knife blades in the sun. Each one held a shield with a silver boss – a single silver sphere on a black field. The four at the front brandished long swords while the others carried torches. They rode purposefully, the leaders striking down any man, woman, child or dog in their way; behind them, the others set light to the thatch of every building they passed. When a man broke free of the burning village, the soldier at the head of the column yelled an order, and instantly a horseman wheeled his mount and turned in pursuit.

Edmund cried out to warn the man, but in an instant he was following too. There was a familiar galloping motion beneath him; he was riding, and in the corner of his eye he caught a glint of metal: a raised sword. Surging through his horror came another feeling – a cold, ferocious pleasure.

The fleeing man had tripped on a boulder and gone sprawling. Edmund bore down on the crouching figure, his sword-arm held high. He could do nothing to stop it. He was caught behind the eyes of the killer, swooping towards his prey.

And although Edmund fought to break free as the sword drew back to strike, it was hopeless. He could not even close his eyes as the blade fell.

CHAPTER FIVE

'Edmund. Wake up!'

The boy was thrashing and moaning in his sleep. He looked so defenceless, Elspeth thought: his arm so pale beneath her sun-burned hand! He was small too, considering her father had said that their shy passenger was about her age. Her heart twisted. Thoughts of her father had kept her awake most of the night, and her eyes felt bruised and raw. So did her right hand, which still twitched and throbbed. When she had finally dozed, she had woken almost at once, her hand clenched on an invisible hilt. Yet when she touched her palm there was nothing there, only a prickling feeling as if something was lying in wait beneath the skin.

By the time a dim oval of sky showed at the cave mouth, she had only one thought.

Medwel, Aagard had called the nearby settlement. The villagers might have seen the shipwreck, might have combed the shore already for whatever the sea had washed up. And they would take in any survivors, he had said.

I don't need to wake the old man, she decided. *If I leave now, I can be there by sun-up, ask about the* Spearwa, *and then, at least, I'll know.*

But she was nagged by an odd sense of responsibility towards the boy. Her father had promised to see him safely to Gaul. And so if there was no news at Medwel – Elspeth's mind shied from the thought – she must take him to the nearest port and find him a boat to Gaul. That would be the right thing to do. Then she must look out for one of the many shipmasters who knew her, and work her passage back to Dubris.

She shook the boy again.

'It's nearly morning,' she whispered, glancing across the cave to where Aagard lay. 'Come on – we need to find a port.'

Edmund gave a great shudder then jerked upright, wild-eyed. 'Murderers! Stop him . . . stop . . .' His voice was a strangled croak.

'Hush!' Elspeth hissed. 'Calm yourself. You've been dreaming.'

Edmund's eyes focused on hers and his breathing slowed. 'Did I cry out?' he whispered. 'I'm sorry. It was just a nightmare.'

'About the storm?' she said quietly.

'No . . . I . . . I don't remember now,' he said.

But Elspeth could see by the pinched look on his face that his dream was still playing itself out behind his eyes. She scrambled to her feet.

'I'm going to Medwel to get news of my father. If there's none there, I'll head back east. I thought you might come with me. I can set you on your way to Gaul.'

'No,' Edmund said, and he spoke so sharply that Elspeth frowned: did he not trust her to finish her father's business? She opened her mouth to object, but he said more gently, 'We can't go without speaking to Aagard. We must thank him, at least.'

Elspeth flushed guiltily. In her rush to be gone, she had forgotten her manners. 'I'll leave him my scaling-knife,' she said. 'In thanks for the lodging. He knows I must find out what's happened to the *Spearwa*!'

'But you must come back here!' Edmund pressed her. 'How else will you find out about the sword?'

'I don't *have* a sword!' she snapped. 'It's gone, and I want no more of it! Aagard can conjure it again for someone else.'

'I fear he cannot do that,' said a voice. Aagard stood above them, looking ghostly in the dawn light. He shook his head, his brow furrowed with concern. 'Edmund is right, child. The sword has chosen you, and it will not change its mind. Nor do I have the power to take it from you. But if you stay here awhile, I can at least help you to discover its purpose, find out why it has returned – and why it has chosen you to bear it.'

As soon as Aagard said this, Elspeth felt the tingling in her right hand, the press of the hilt in her palm. She made a fist to crush it, and glared at the man.

'The sword needs to choose someone else!' she cried. The old man looked so kindly at her that Elspeth's eyes pricked with tears. 'I'm sorry, sir,' she mumbled. 'You've been good to me, and I have little to repay you. I'll give the sword back . . . for how can I use it? I'm a seafarer not a soldier.' She wiped the tears away. 'And I have to find my father. If he's not in Medwel, I must return to Kent and tell the people in Dubris what has happened.'

But Aagard was turning to Edmund. 'And you?' he prompted. 'Are you set on going also? Your gift is no more welcome, but if you wish to stay here, I will help you with it as much I can.'

Elspeth frowned. What gift? What did the boy have? She saw Edmund stiffen, his pale face translucent with strain. When he spoke there was a hint of the old haughtiness, though his tone was polite.

'Thank you, sir. I am most grateful to you. But I must leave too. I have family in Noviomagus. They will think I am dead when news of the shipwreck reaches them.'

Aagard sighed. 'I wish I could change your minds,' he said gravely. 'I fear you are going into more danger than you know. Your destinies will follow you both no matter where you go. But perhaps it is best for you to return to your homes first.' He walked across the cave to two big storage jars. Elspeth saw him scoop a handful from each into skin bags. 'We had better stock up for the journey,' he muttered, half to himself. 'I'll go with you as far as I can, but from then, your gods and your God will have to watch over you.'

*

The sun was a bright line on the horizon as they descended the coastal path to Medwel. Aagard took the lead, neither age nor the rocky track slowing his steps. On their right hand the sea spread below them, calmer now and lapping at the sand like the tongue of a patient dog. Already the last night's storm seemed beyond belief, as hard to recall as a distant nightmare.

Aagard had given Edmund and Elspeth a bag each of dried fish and barley bread and their blankets from the night before. When Elspeth tried to give him her knife in payment, the old man had waved it away. Edmund had felt deeply ashamed because he didn't even have a knife to offer. He gritted his teeth. Nothing was the same since he set sail on the *Spearwa*.

I should have told Aagard about the dream. It seemed so real – the village, the fire, the soldiers, the callous slaughter, that man I killed – Edmund's heart banged against his ribs as the sense of savage joy surged once more in his mind. Gods save him! It was the same feeling he'd had looking down on the foundering *Spearwa*. The same flood of cruel pleasure when he'd watched through the dragon's eyes . . .

Edmund clenched his fists. No! He would not even think the word. He noticed Elspeth watching him with a worried look. Curse her, she was always watching him. He quickly bent down to pull a gorse thorn from his leggings. He couldn't let her see him being cowardly again, not like on the ship. He was a king's son. What if they could see him now in his father's great hall? Edmund the Puny! Edmund the Frightened Mouse!

He took a deep breath as his Uncle Aelfred had taught him

years ago, when he had woken from a screaming nightmare. 'Remember, little Whitewing, if you pretend to be brave,' Aelfred had said, 'you will *be* brave!'

Edmund straightened his bruised back and squared his shoulders. He had survived the storm, the shipwreck, the dragon, the savage sea. Now he had to go home as fast as he could so his mother would not fret over his death.

He set off again with a more determined stride.

At last they reached the top and rounded the headland. But when Edmund saw the village huts strung out above the stony bay, dread rolled back like a tidal wave. He heard Aagard call out 'Medwel', but whatever else the old man said was lost in the roaring inside Edmund's head.

It was the village from his dream! There were the thatched houses encircling the green, with fish-drying huts in the middle and scrubland all around. Below the settlement a pebbled beach sloped down to the sea, where several small craft were hauled up high above the tideline. It was almost impossible to imagine fire and slaughter riding on iron-shod horses in this wild, beautiful place. But Edmund had *seen* it happen!

As the path widened, Elspeth ran past Aagard towards the village. The old man quickened his pace behind her, as if fearful of the news that might greet her. Edmund stumbled after them, his head filled with nothing but images of torch-bearing riders and soldiers wielding swords on defenceless men.

But inside the village, all was peaceful. There was a whiff of fish from the drying-sheds. Outside their doors, women were gutting and splitting herring. A pot of gruel bubbled at a communal hearth. On the scrubby patch of grass amid the houses, a clutch of bare-legged children hooted and rolled with two scrawny puppies.

When Edmund caught up with the others, Aagard was talking to a ruddy-faced woman. He heard her say, 'Hale and hearty as ever was. And all thanks to your good healing, Master Aagard. We thought we'd lost our babby for sure.'

Her words washed over Edmund.

This can't be the place I saw. There's no danger here. They'll think me a madman if I start blabbing about raiders.

A shout from the woman jerked him from his thoughts.

'Last night! The two of you came out of the storm unharmed? Well I nev—'

Elspeth broke in impatiently. 'Have you found anyone else? Did anyone wash up here alive?'

The woman looked at her in astonishment. 'Alive? Why, we've scarcely found a splinter of wood to light a fire! Nor even a drowned body so far.' Reading grief beyond words in Elspeth's stricken expression, she added hastily, 'But you could ask the menfolk, they were still out searching this morning . . .' Her voice trailed off, but Elspeth was already running down to the beach.

Aagard looked as if he longed to stop her, as if he knew there was no point, that only two of them had survived the storm and the sinking of the *Spearwa*. Instead he said to

Edmund, 'We should move on as soon as we can. If the sword shows itself in the open, there will be danger for both of you.'

Edmund stared at him. It was not for Aagard to tell him when to travel; it was not for Aagard to tell him he was at risk because an enchanted sword had somehow attached itself to the boat-girl's hand. If the danger was that great, Edmund should travel alone. He had a kingless court waiting for him.

He opened his mouth to argue, then shut it again. He would be no more use on his own than a damp kit. His mind was befuddled with dreams; he did not know which way to go, and most of all, he was scared. Scared by the storm, scared by the visions of sword-bearing men on horses, and scared of the dragon he had seen in the sky.

Elspeth dragged herself back from the beach, her legs sinking into the shingle with every step. The fishermen she had spoken to had seen no sign of a survivor from the *Spearwa*. One old man reported that the ship had burned as it sank, and what wreckage had been washed ashore was blackened and charred.

''Twas the biggest mystery for sure, young miss,' he had said, 'that a fire could have raged in seas like that. But flames there were, hotter than a forging fire by the look of the wood.' He was amazed that Elspeth had escaped the wreck. All the fishermen had looked at her with awe in their eyes. And even a hint of fear, as if they suspected her of being a mermaid or a sea-sprite. There could be no other survivors, they were sure.

Offering clumsy thanks, Elspeth turned blindly back to the village, her eyes brimming with tears. But by the time she reached the houses, the tears had blown away. What use was crying? She had nothing left but the port she called home, and she would need all of her strength for the long journey east.

Aagard greeted her without comment, though she could see at once that he knew, and she was glad that he asked her no questions. Edmund said nothing either. He was tense and white as sea spume. Neither of them offered any objection when the woman whose baby Aagard had saved invited them to eat with her.

Elspeth sat by the fire pit in the woman's cramped hut, chewing an oatcake without tasting it and letting the talk drift over her.

'The road eastwards is well marked, and safe enough if a traveller keeps to it,' Aagard was saying. 'Or it was, two years ago. And there are those in Wessex who will offer us shelter. We will leave as soon as we have eaten.'

Elspeth wondered what she would do when she reached Dubris. Her father's house was small and bare; his real home, all his wealth, had been the *Spearwa*. Aunt Freda, her father's sister and Elspeth's only other living relative, would take her in, but her house was already full with three girls who sewed and spun and giggled about husbands. *No!* Elspeth couldn't stay there. The only place she could really be happy was at sea. She would find a Dubris shipmaster to take her on;

someone who knew Master Trymman had schooled his daughter well.

There was something else too. She had to go home to find out for certain that her father hadn't found his way there by some other means. If she had been saved by a piece of jetsam, then why not he? Didn't he always, always go home to Dubris, a fair wind filling his sails as he tacked round the point into Dubris harbour?

The pain in Elspeth's heart lightened a little. Aagard's speculation about the state of the roads was of no importance to her. She had to head for the nearest port. It seemed the boy no longer meant to go to Gaul, so she did not have to worry about that either. Perhaps they could travel east together by boat.

Elspeth glanced across the gloomy little hut to the pale boy. Would he want to go with her? Maybe not. He was so reserved, so caught up in his private thoughts it was as if it would harm him to speak out loud.

She was surprised when he suddenly stood up and faced Aagard, his jaw set as if he had made up his mind to do some difficult task. He fumbled at his throat with trembling fingers.

'P-please take this, sir,' he stammered. 'I-it will go some way towards repaying your hospitality.'

As Aagard took the small object, his grizzled brows shot up. Elspeth saw a silver clasp in his palm, shaped like a flying bird.

Aagard handed the clasp back to the boy. 'It would repay me many times over,' he said, 'but this is too rich a gift. Keep it, Edmund, and keep it hidden. The gratitude of your family is no small thing, I know that.'

To Elspeth's growing confusion, Edmund turned redder than a radish, and took back the clasp without a word.

As they left Medwel, Elspeth ran to catch up with Aagard.

'Sir,' she said, 'I cannot come with you. I have decided to go home by boat. I must find the nearest port and a ship-master who knows me.'

Aagard turned on her. 'No!' he said fiercely, and before Elspeth could protest, he seized her by the shoulders. 'You must *not* go by sea,' he said. 'Neither one of you. You must realise that you have enemies now, and the sea routes are watched. There were eyes in that storm.'

Elspeth felt the ground sway beneath her. 'But how can I not go back to sea? There's nothing else . . .' Her voice tailed off.

Aagard's eyes flashed. 'Trust yourself to a ship again,' he said, 'and the dragon will find you. He is conjured in storm and there is no escape for you at sea. Look what happened to your ship. Hardly a timber left. At least on land, there are places to hide, and people to help you.'

Dragon? Elspeth frowned. Had she had heard him aright? She glanced at Edmund, and was astounded to see he was nodding.

'He's right, Elspeth,' he said. 'We have to travel by land.'

Elspeth stared numbly at him. A dragon meant to hunt her from the sea? And Aagard and Edmund believed this? The sea was the only life she knew. If she could not have that, what did she have left?

Suddenly a jolt of cold power raced up her arm. For an instant she felt the silver gauntlet on her hand, the weight of the invisible sword hilt in her grasp. And a voice deep inside her head whispered:

You have me, Elspeth. You have me.

CHAPTER SIX

By sunset they had travelled several leagues from the coast. At Edmund's side, Elspeth trudged in silence as if each step dragged at her heart. He felt a stab of sympathy for the girl, noticing the way she repeatedly rubbed her right hand. Whatever enchantment had made the sword come and go, it had clearly left some trace on her skin.

Edmund decided she was owed more explanation about the danger they were in than he and Aagard had given her, but he did not know how to start. Haltingly, he told her about his vision in the storm and the old man's account of the dragon, Torment. But of his newly discovered power, he said very little. He still could not even bring himself to utter the word Ripente, let alone believe he was one. As he spoke, he was relieved to see Elspeth tilt her head to listen, as if she believed what he was saying and knew that she couldn't shut herself off in her grief and pretend there were no such things as dragons.

'Aagard is right about the danger being greater at sea,'

Edmund concluded. 'I wouldn't trust to a ship again – not along this coast, anyway.'

'But you were meant to sail to Gaul,' Elspeth remembered. 'Your father wanted you to join him there. Will you not go at all now?'

Edmund shook his head. 'I must go home to Sussex,' he said. 'My mother will hear about the wreck, and I need to let her know that I'm still alive.' There was something else too. The dream of pillaging soldiers flooded Edmund's mind, and even though they had not been the Viking raiders that threatened his home to the west, he knew his mother's decision to send him away had been wrong. He should not have left her to face the threat of raiders alone. But he could not tell Elspeth this without giving away more than he wanted about his true identity, so he quickly steered the conversation away from himself.

'And you?' he asked. 'Will you stay in your father's village?'

Elspeth smiled bleakly. 'It's the place I know best . . . on land.' She did not seem willing to say anything else about her plans, so Edmund let her walk ahead as the path narrowed and fell back to look at the unfamiliar countryside around them.

The coarse clifftop scrubland around Medwel had given way to well-kept fields. When they were walking three abreast again along the edge of a field of clover, Aagard announced that they would spend the night at the settlement of a friend of his, a local thane named Gilbert.

'He owns a dozen hides of land hereabouts,' Aagard explained, as they approached the tall wooden palisade surrounding the village.

The men at the gate welcomed Aagard in, and Gilbert himself, a big, fair-bearded man, seemed more than pleased to see him. The thane led them past the crudely thatched homes of slaves and bondsmen, and past workshops and storerooms, to his longhouse. It was a narrow, rectangular building many times bigger than any in Medwel. Inside, Gilbert's household was already at supper, sitting at two long tables made from broad planks of wood resting on sheaves of straw.

'Radegund!' Gilbert called. 'We have three more guests! Aagard is here, and two poor souls he rescued from that shipwreck two nights ago.'

The lady of the house looked up from the pot she was stirring and sent a slave girl scurrying off for more salt pork.

'We're honoured with guests today!' she told Aagard, gesturing him towards one of the tables where some seats were still empty. Two burly men looked up as she passed; Radegund introduced them as Deor and Dagobert, brothers who were returning west from a trading expedition. At the far end of the table another guest nodded to Aagard. He was a small, sharp-featured man, neither old nor young, lean and compact in frame and dressed plainly for travel. He glanced incuriously at Edmund and Elspeth as they approached, but as his gaze passed over them, Edmund felt the man read him like a book; as if his ancestry, past and future had been written on his face.

Aagard stopped to greet the stranger. 'Well met, Cluaran,' he said. His tone was cordial, but Edmund detected a cautious edge as he added, 'I wondered if you might be here.' He turned to Elspeth and Edmund. 'This is Cluaran. He –'

'I'm a traveller, a dealer in old scraps,' interrupted the man in a light, musical voice. He had a lilting accent, unlike any that Edmund had heard before. 'I pick up odd fragments of songs and stories and pass them on in return for my supper. I'm honoured to meet you, lady, young sir.' He bowed his head humbly, but Edmund caught a gleam of mockery in his grey-green eyes.

'Cluaran is a minstrel, and a fine one,' their hostess told them, serving them with bowls of barley broth. 'He comes here every year with his songs and all the news of the kingdoms. You've come at a good time. There'll be merry-making tonight!'

Edmund was used to dining at his father's court, but he had to admit that Gilbert was a generous host. He saw Elspeth's eyes widen at the sight of the heaped platters of bread and meat; saw her nod speechlessly when a slave came around with a wine flask.

'Be careful!' Edmund warned as she took up her cup. 'It's strong stuff if you've not had it before – it's not like ale.' But he was too late; Elspeth had already taken a deep draught. She spluttered and dropped the cup, sending the golden liquid splashing across the table. The two trader brothers sitting opposite drew back in exaggerated alarm.

'No need to throw it away, girl, if you don't like it!' called one, while his brother sniggered.

Elspeth stared down at the table, her cheeks turning scarlet. Edmund waved a hand to summon the nearest slave girl, and as she mopped the spilled wine he gave the smirking men a look that he had once seen his father using on an ill-mannered messenger. It did not have quite the quelling effect Edmund remembered, but both men gave him uneasy glances and turned back to their food.

'My thanks for the warning,' Elspeth whispered wryly when the slave girl had gone. 'But where have you been, that you've drunk wine? No one that I know drinks anything other than ale and milk.'

Edmund was saved from having to answer by the minstrel, Cluaran. The tables fell silent as he took up his harp and began to play: first a lively catch that set everyone clapping and shouting, then the sad strains of 'The Wanderer's Lament'. By the time the slaves came to clear away the empty platters, he was half-chanting, half-singing the tale of 'The Booty of Annwvyn'. Edmund knew the story well from his mother, but he was transfixed by the man's strange, soft-pitched voice. Even Elspeth smiled as the minstrel sang of the giant who was mistaken for a mountain and the quest for a cauldron which brought the dead to life. Gilbert roared his approval and sent over more warmed ale for the singer.

Finally the minstrel laid down his harp to a general cry of disappointment. Edmund watched the man curiously. He was undoubtedly popular, but no one went to praise the minstrel's performance to his face; nor did he seek anyone's company. He sat alone on an upturned barrel at the end of the table, drinking his ale in silence. Only Aagard, after a while, went over and talked with him briefly.

'Is Cluaran a friend of yours?' Edmund asked when the old man returned.

Aagard did not reply at once. When he did, he seemed to frame his words very carefully. 'He has been of help to me in the past,' he said. 'And I to him, I believe. He can be a good ally in time of need. But no, I would not call Cluaran a friend.'

The minstrel ate alone the next morning as well. Edmund saw him sitting on the far side of the fire while the trader brothers ate at the table with some men of the household, all talking cheerfully. He, Elspeth and Aagard were seated with their host. Gilbert had been at pains to make them welcome; they had been given good straw beds in the hall itself, where the fire was kept burning low all night, and offered as much bread and cheese as they could eat for breakfast. The thane seemed sorry when Aagard told him they planned to leave, and shook his head to hear where they were going.

'You know your own mind of course, Master Aagard,' he said, 'but you'll have a long walk to get these two youngsters back home, and there are sorry tales coming out of Wessex lately, tales of lawlessness beyond ordinary thieves. They say King Beotrich's own men go about demanding tribute from all and sundry, and no one stops them.'

'So Cluaran told me last night,' Aagard said, his tone bleak. 'Yet we must go.'

Gilbert's broad face brightened. 'Why not travel with the minstrel? He's headed for Wareham; that's on your way, more or less. He's known in thanes' houses across the land. He could vouch for you, where you'll be a stranger.'

'Cluaran travels alone,' said Aagard, glancing over to where the man sat at his meal, ignoring all around him. 'He would not welcome company.' But there was something about the old man's look that suggested he was not altogether decided in this.

They were ready to go as soon as they had eaten. As Aagard took his leave of Gilbert, Edmund hovered at the door, anxious to be off. He saw Cluaran striding towards the gate with his pack and harp case on his back; heading out alone, as Aagard had said. Edmund was not sorry to see the man go. He had not liked that penetrating look when they had met the minstrel for the first time. Besides, he wanted to take the fastest route home, not travel on some minstrel's route from house to house.

As they left the stockade, a man on horseback was spurring his sweating horse up the coastal road towards the settlement.

Aagard stopped in the gateway. 'Wait here a moment,' he

told Edmund and Elspeth, and walked back through the gate. Edmund heard him calling to someone, and a few moments later he returned with Gilbert puffing after him.

'Hey, Wulf!' Gilbert called to the rider. 'What's spooked you?' He broke off, his eyes widening in alarm. Wulf's face was deathly pale, and a long cut ran down one cheek.

'Medwel!' the man gasped as he yanked his horse to a halt.

Edmund went cold. Aagard and Gilbert ran to help Wulf dismount, but even when Elspeth tugged at his arm, his legs would not move.

'I must go back! We must all go!' the man protested. 'There are armed men attacking with torches. Medwel is burning!'

Edmund cried out. But no one seemed to hear as Gilbert bellowed for his men-at-arms. Aagard urgently questioned the man about what he had seen. The words came to Edmund dimly: '. . . some lord's men, armed with swords, not common raiders. They were demanding something from the elders, I never heard what. When they started burning the houses, I came to fetch help.'

Edmund did not want to hear. The sight of the blazing thatch, the screaming people, came so vividly to his mind that he fell to his knees, throwing his arms over his head.

'Edmund?'

Aagard was standing over him while Gilbert's men rushed around gathering spears, saddling horses. Edmund knew it would take them at least an hour's riding to reach Medwel. He knew that Gilbert, as thane, was bound to do what he could. But he could not watch the rescue party gather, nor look at Aagard's face. He felt sick.

'Edmund,' the old man said again. 'What ails you, boy?'

'I saw it,' Edmund murmured. And when Aagard seemed slow to understand, he cried angrily, 'I saw them attacking Medwel! Armed men, just as Wulf said, all dressed alike. They had silver bosses on their shields.' He stopped. He could not talk about the way they had mown down the people in their path, as coolly as a boy slashing wheat stalks. Nor about the way he had slashed too, revelling in the slice of steel through air. And bone.

Both Aagard and Elspeth were staring at him now.

'But how could you know?' Elspeth began.

Aagard hushed her with a gesture. His face was like stone, his eyes fixed on Edmund's as he waited for him to continue.

'Before we left the cave I had a dream,' Edmund told them haltingly. 'When we passed through Medwel yesterday I knew it was the same place, but it was so quiet, so peaceful. I said nothing about what I had seen. I thought no one would believe me.'

'I would have believed you, Edmund,' Aagard said quietly. 'You spoke of men with a silver sphere on black shields?' When Edmund nodded, the old man frowned. 'I have known only one man who wore a shield mark like that. Orgrim.'

Edmund gazed at him, bewildered. 'But why would he send men to burn Medwel?'

Instead of answering, Aagard froze for a moment. Then he

flung up his arms to hide his face. 'He is trying to use my eyes!' he cried. 'Close your eyes, both of you!'

Edmund did as he was told. The panic in the old man's voice had chilled him to the bone.

'Did I not say he was Ripente?' Aagard muttered. 'I felt him looking through my eyes – trying to see who was with me, who had survived the shipwreck.'

Edmund stared into darkness, his mind racing. Was Orgrim stealing into his mind that very second? How could Aagard tell?

But then he felt it. Something squeezed inside his head, as if the edge of his mind had been pushed aside. Almost at once the pressure was gone, but he was still aware of *something*: an absence like a hole in his thoughts. Carefully, as if probing a loose tooth, he felt for it again.

Then it hit him: a rush of consciousness that was not his own, chill and scouring as a snow-wind. There was malice too, the will to seize, make use of and then discard. It swelled to fill his whole head. Edmund fought back, but it was like pushing against a mist. Steadily his thoughts grew fainter and fainter, until they were little more than wisps of cloud blown in a windy sky.

With a distant sense of horror, Edmund felt himself dissolve.

CHAPTER SEVEN

Edmund felt Aagard's steadying hand on his shoulder.

'You can sense him, then.' The old man's voice seemed far away. 'He cannot control you, nor hear you, Edmund. Try to close your mind to him!'

Edmund tried again to push back the invading presence. How could he shut it out? Perhaps if he could find the source . . .

Yes. There was an opening in the smooth, curved wall of his mind, and something not quite liquid was pouring through the gap like smoke. Edmund gathered his last ounce of purpose and tried to stop the gap.

Slowly, the other mind withdrew. Only the sense of malice remained – an evil gloating that said that although it was leaving now, it might soon return. And then it too faded, and the rip in Edmund's mind closed up.

Edmund slumped against the fence, Aagard's hand still on his shoulder. Elspeth looked from one to the other.

'What happened?' she demanded.

'Orgrim tried to use Edmund's eyes,' Aagard said. His face seemed more lined than ever. 'He reached out to me first. He has done so enough times that I know the touch of his mind. When I closed my eyes, he tried to use Edmund, probably because he looked young enough to overpower.'

'But why?' Elspeth pleaded, shuddering at the thought of someone else inside her head, looking out through her eyes. 'Why does he want to look through our eyes?'

Aagard looked solemn. 'Because he is hunting the crystal sword.'

Elspeth frowned. 'But I felt nothing,' she said. Involuntarily she glanced down at her hand. If Orgrim wanted to find the sword, why not try the person who held it now?

'It's possible that the sword protects you,' said the old man, looking at her thoughtfully. 'On the other hand, most of those touched by the Ripente know nothing about it. I have studied hard, so I may feel the signs, but I could never do what Edmund has just done, and fight him off when he had taken hold of my mind.' He turned to Edmund. 'I had heard that one Ripente can drive out another.'

'I don't know,' Edmund said. 'It . . . he . . . left me alone. I saw the gap in my mind, but I don't think I drove him out.' He looked drained, as if talking was an effort.

'You fought him,' Aagard said with quiet certainty. 'You recognised his presence at once, and you were able to combat him. In time, you will learn to defeat him altogether.'

'You mean he really will come back?' Edmund groaned. '*Why?* Even if I have the same skill, I'm nothing to him!'

'He has seen you with me,' Aagard explained. 'And he will wonder what I have told you about the chest. Perhaps I have drawn attention to you by accompanying you this far. But that cannot be helped now. Orgrim's power is growing. The book of spells has taught him to conjure dragons, and he brought the storm that sank your ship. He must have known the crystal sword was aboard, and he wanted to prevent it from reaching Gaul.'

Elspeth shook her head in disbelief. She wanted to shout: *You mean Orgrim will be hunting me now? Then take the sword back! I did not choose any of this!* She looked down in dismay at her hand and felt the gauntlet's grip, the hilt's cold pulse. Again she clenched her fist, crushing them to bits.

'Master Aagard.'

Gilbert was running up to them, his broad face anxious. 'We're riding now for Medwel,' he said, gesturing to the armed and mounted men behind him. 'Will you come with us? I fear your skill at healing will be much needed.'

Elspeth saw Aagard's face darken. 'I will come and do what I can,' he said to Gilbert. Then he turned to Elspeth and Edmund. 'You must go on, both of you. If Orgrim's men are this close, you are in even greater danger than I first thought.' His eyes narrowed as he looked at Elspeth. 'Are you really set on returning to your village? It might be safer for you to head south into Dunmonia, hide there until the heat of the chase has cooled.'

'Hide?' Elspeth echoed in dismay. 'Never! I did not choose the sword. This sorcerer can have no quarrel with me! I'm going back to Dubris.' Aagard had forbidden her the sea. He could not banish her from her father's house as well!

The old man sighed. 'Then the two of you must travel east together. To reach Sussex and Kent you will have to go through Wessex, towards the very danger that you must avoid. Orgrim holds sway over the entire kingdom, and the road runs right through Venta Bulgarum, his stronghold. You must skirt the town, and on no account enter it.' He hesitated. 'Perhaps I should go with you –'

'No!' Edmund argued, and Elspeth was surprised by the note of command in his voice. Wherever Edmund came from, he must live in a longhouse at least as big as Gilbert's. Perhaps he even had slaves to pour his wine as well. 'You must go back to Medwel,' Edmund insisted. 'They need you! It's my fault they were unprepared for the raid, and I cannot let you abandon them again.'

'We will have urgent need of you, Master Aagard,' Lord Gilbert agreed. 'Send the young ones after Cluaran, if you think they'll go astray on their own. He's not long gone – they'll catch him easily.'

Edmund shook his head. 'We'll be fine on our own.'

Elspeth wasn't sure she agreed. If Aagard was right about the amount of danger they were in, they would surely be safer travelling with someone who knew the roads? Her right arm and hand began throbbing again, distracting her thoughts. *Leave me alone!* she told the sword.

'If I go,' Aagard said at last, 'you must promise me that you will find Cluaran and tell him I have charged him with your protection.'

'Charged him?' Edmund protested. 'We don't need –'

'Swear it!' Aagard insisted. 'Tell him I demanded this in the name of the one who never died. He will understand. If he hears that, he will not desert you.'

Edmund looked mutinous, and Elspeth's irritation boiled over. 'Do you want Aagard to go to Medwel or not?' she hissed at him. She turned to Aagard. 'We promise,' she said. Beside her, Edmund nodded crossly.

Aagard saluted Gilbert. 'I will ride with you, my lord.' He clasped Elspeth's and Edmund's hands once more. 'You must go at once,' he urged. 'Remember your promise, and trust no one but each other – not even Cluaran, unless it is to guide you on your journey. When I have learned more of Orgrim's plans, I can find you in Noviomagus and Dubris, or send Thrimgar to you. Go safely. And may your gods and your God speed you.'

He gave them one last look, then turned and strode to the horse that was held ready for him. Moments later Gilbert and his men were galloping away to the south, and Elspeth and Edmund were left alone in the gateway.

*

Elspeth stood with Edmund on a little ridge outside the village, looking down on the distant, north-eastern road. The morning was fine, but the spring sunlight felt weak and the breeze cool. The sky stretched vastly above them, hanging over land that looked neither familiar nor welcoming to Elspeth's sea-trained eyes. Instinctively her left hand went to her right, which still tingled with an itch beneath the skin.

'We had better catch up with Cluaran, then,' she said.

Edmund shrugged. 'If that's what you want.' He added bad-temperedly, 'I don't know why Aagard made us promise to ask for his protection. I don't want protection from some stranger Aagard doesn't even call a friend.'

His lofty tone grated on Elspeth, but when she looked at him she saw only distress in his eyes. She wondered if he was as nervous as she was at the journey ahead and if, like her, he felt burdened by his strange, unasked-for gift.

They scrambled down the slippery slopes of the ridge to the road. On either side lay sparse meadowland with a few stunted trees at the edge, their new buds barely broken. The road itself was little more than a track, stony and rutted, but it ran straight, and the narrow footprints that appeared here and there showed that Cluaran was still ahead.

Elspeth was glad to be on the move again. *When I get back to Dubris, I'll go straight back to sea,* she decided. *And if this dragon that Edmund saw is still threatening the south coast, then I'll take a ship to Northumbria, or even up to Hibernia.*

But there was still so far to go – two kingdoms to cross. They would have to go near Venta Bulgarum, if not through it, and Elspeth knew this was dangerous. Whenever Aagard mentioned the town, her arm had tingled with that strange energy.

Elspeth frowned. The enchanted sword seemed to have some purpose of its own, quite outside her own plans. But Venta was a town like any other, she told herself, and her quickest route home lay through it. She would not be put off by omens from an invisible sword.

She glanced over her shoulder. Edmund was trailing behind, staring dismally at the dusty road beneath his feet. Perhaps she should make more effort to befriend him. They had endured so much in the last two days, more death and destruction than most people saw in a lifetime. Elspeth's world been had turned on its head – her father gone, the *Spearwa* gone – and in their place only outlandish talk of unnatural storms and conjured dragons, Ripente visions, and the blackest sorcery.

Elspeth sighed. Whatever else was going on in this turned-up world, to walk in silence all the way from Dunmonia to Sussex would be terribly tedious. She shortened her stride, and smiled as Edmund caught her up.

'You said you're from Sussex?' she began.

'My family live in Noviomagus,' he said stiffly.

'Do you have brothers or sisters?'

Elspeth was prepared to be interested, even envious. When Edmund had told Aagard his family would worry about him, she had pictured a whole clan longing for his return. She was taken aback when he glared at her.

'Why do you want to know?' he snapped.

'I thought you were lucky to *have* a family, that's all!' she cried. 'That there's someone who cares if you live or die.'

He walked on without replying, staring straight ahead.

'Are you going to be like this all the way?' she demanded, running after him. 'It's plain to see you're some lord's son, with your silver brooch and your lofty airs – but does that mean I'm not even allowed to speak to you?'

Edmund stopped dead, then turned on her, his eyes bleak. 'I'm a king's son,' he said.

Elspeth stared at him as he went on in strained tones. 'The silver clasp you saw is my name-brooch. It belonged to my father, Heored, King of Sussex.'

Elspeth remembered Edmund's aloofness on the *Spearwa*, his confident poise in the thane's great house – he had drunk wine all his life, of course – and his constant air of secrecy. So that was why . . . She realised she'd been gaping like a fish.

'But why did he send you away on my father's ship?'

'For safety,' Edmund said harshly. 'My father's cousin in Mercia sent word that his lands were being threatened by the Danish invaders, and my father took all the good men of the kingdom and rode to help him, leaving my mother to rule in his place. That was months ago, and we've heard no word from them since. Then the Danes attacked our coast.' He frowned. 'My mother wanted me to go to her brother Aelfred in Gaul. I was to stay there until the danger was over. That way, she said, I could return to rule the kingdom if . . . if there was no one else.' His voice was low and hard, but Elspeth caught a flicker of misery in the boy's face.

'And would your uncle have made you welcome?' she asked gently, thinking of her aunt's overcrowded household in Dubris.

'I think so. He lived in my father's house when I was small. I was fond of him, and he of me. He went to Gaul to make his fortune and never returned, but he sent letters asking me and my mother to visit him.' Edmund's face clouded with memory, then hardened again. 'But it makes no difference now. My mother will hear of the wreck and think me dead. I have to go back. I should never have left.'

'We'd best get on with the journey, then,' Elspeth said briskly. 'Maybe we can reach your mother before the news does.'

Edmund had not moved. 'Elspeth.' His voice was suddenly urgent. 'If we have to travel with this Cluaran, he mustn't know who I am! The sons of lords have been kidnapped many times before now, and held for ransom. Promise me you'll say nothing.'

He was an odd boy, Elspeth thought: so stiff and haughty one minute, then so fearful the next. But it was a small thing to ask in return for peace on the journey.

'Agreed,' she said. 'Now come on, or we'll never catch him.'

The road climbed ahead of them, the trees giving way to gorse and heather. At the top of the next rise they caught sight of a small figure heading eastwards, and they quickened their pace to catch up with him. Several times as the day wore on, they seemed to be drawing nearer to the brown-clad figure, only to lose sight of him and spot him again as far away as ever.

The shadows were beginning to lengthen when Elspeth touched Edmund's arm and gestured to him to listen. They were in upland country of rocks and heath; there were no trees and only an occasional bird call. But as a breeze blew along the track towards them they could faintly hear a man's voice, raised in song.

'We're near him!' she said.

But even though they quickened their pace, by dusk they still had not caught up with him. When they could no longer see the track in front of them, Edmund said, 'We'd better stop for the night.'

Elspeth nodded, her teeth chattering. They found a rocky outcrop that gave them a little shelter, and sat back-to-back on the prickly turf, hugging the blankets that Aagard had given them. It was too cold for sleep. They munched bread from their supplies and stared gloomily into the darkness.

Suddenly Edmund spotted a flickering orange glow in the distance, and at the same moment Elspeth raised her head and sniffed.

'I smell smoke!'

Without another word they rose, each clutching a blanket, and made their way towards the fire.

Cluaran was sitting beyond the next bend of the road at a small campfire, his back towards them. Before they reached the circle of warmth, he lifted his harp out of its case and began to play.

Edmund and Elspeth stopped to listen. The singer seemed to be addressing someone, his voice now swooping in heart-rending cadence, now almost speaking, though neither Edmund nor Elspeth understood the words. When Cluaran finally stopped and laid down his harp, he spoke a few more quiet words in the unknown language. Then, without turning his head, the minstrel said, 'You may as well come sit by the fire, both of you. It's a bitter night, and there's room enough for three.'

CHAPTER EIGHT

Edmund lay curled in the warmth cast by the flames, listening to Elspeth's steady breathing as she slept beside him. The minstrel had been happy to share his fire, but he'd made it clear at once that it was for that night only.

'We'll go our separate ways in the morning,' Cluaran had told them. 'I've no time to watch over children.'

'But –' Elspeth had begun, and Edmund had kicked her ankle to silence her. It had been all he could do not to walk off into the night, icy wind or no. *Watch over children!*

Cluaran's words still rankled. What right had this stranger to speak of them so contemptuously? They had survived shipwreck and murder. Edmund had used the eyes of a dragon, and Elspeth held in her hand an enchanted sword – and this vagabond minstrel was dismissing them as nothing more than infants.

A movement on the other side of the fire caught his attention. Cluaran was slipping away from the circle of yellow light. Edmund felt another rush of anger; was the man planning to abandon them already? But then he saw the minstrel's pack still lying in the grass, just visible at the edge of the firelight.

Edmund rolled on to his back and stared at the half-risen moon. His eyes began to close at last, but the moon's pale light seemed to penetrate his eyelids, finding its way into fitful dreams of dragons, armed men and a sword that glowed like a star.

He woke with a jump. The moon was higher now and he blinked in the pale radiance, trying to catch the threads of his dream again. It was driven abruptly from his mind by the sound of a stealthy tread on the track behind them.

So the minstrel's come back, he thought. Still half-asleep, he let his mind reach out towards the soft footsteps. It felt so natural, so treacherously easy. All he had to do was blink, and when he opened his eyes again, he would be approaching two figures sleeping by a fire . . .

When he realised what he was doing, he recoiled, hot with shame – but at that moment he glimpsed what the other eyes were seeing: a dark figure, moving alongside him.

Edmund jolted awake in an instant. This wasn't Cluaran! There were *two* people approaching. He felt them drawing nearer, slowly and stealthily.

Urgently, he searched again for the eyes he had borrowed. There: he could see more clearly now. The minstrel's campfire was a distant gleam about a hundred paces away. The two humps beside it – himself and Elspeth – were dimly lit by the

82

red flames. But the watcher knew them, somehow; had been expecting to see them.

It was a man. He turned to whisper something to his companion, and Edmund flinched with surprise – whether it was his own body that stirred or the other's, he could not tell. The second figure was one of those trader brothers they had met at Lord Gilbert's home; Dagobert, that was it. Edmund caught a sense of breathless stealth, and overweening greed, and knew these visitors brought trouble.

Very slowly, he reached out a hand to shake Elspeth. 'Wake up!' he whispered.

She stirred, and her eyes snapped open. 'What is it?'

'Thieves,' Edmund breathed.

'Where's Cluaran?'

'Gone off somewhere. If we can get to the other side of the fire, there might be a weapon in his pack.' Edmund sensed the men moving towards them with more urgency now. They were almost within the circle of firelight. 'Ready?' he mouthed. Elspeth nodded.

He took a deep breath, then gripped her arm: *Now!* He jumped to his feet and they sprinted around the fire. From the road he heard hoarse cries as the two men broke into a run. He dived on Cluaran's leather pack and pulled it open: clothing, skins and packages, but nothing they could use to defend themselves. The minstrel had taken his bow with him. Beside him, Elspeth had drawn her little knife and was pulling a big branch from Cluaran's pile of firewood.

'Torches!' he hissed. She nodded, quickly slicing a strip of her tunic hem and wrapping it round the end of a branch. Edmund took it and thrust the cloth end into the fire, stirring up a cloud of smoke as it smouldered.

The two thieves were suddenly huge figures, looming through the smoke.

'You're sure they've no weapons?' one of them muttered.

'You saw for yourself when they left, lackwit!' scoffed the other. He called hoarsely across the fire. 'Hey, you there, lad! Hand over your packs and we'll not hurt you.'

Edmund said nothing. Beside him Elspeth was fumbling, trying to light another torch. He felt her tremble. Suddenly his own torch flared. *Pretend to be brave and you will be brave!* Edmund hoisted the flaming branch as if it was a fine Noviomagus blade. With a yell that he hoped was warlike, he darted around the fire towards the men, brandishing the torch with both hands. The thieves jumped back, but when they saw they faced only a boy with a torch, they laughed and advanced again. In their hands, the firelight glanced off two long knives.

Edmund swiped at the nearest brother with the torch. The thief staggered back, cursing. But the dagger was still in his hand.

Edmund swung at the second man, but he too dodged. Edmund charged again, howling with fury, whirling his torch above his head. This time he felt it strike against something. The thief screamed, beating at his burning left arm with his dagger-hand. Edmund leaped forward – and his torch died.

The first man saw his chance and ran at Edmund with a snarl – just as the second thief doused his burning sleeve and came back to join the fray. The world shrank to two knife-points gleaming in Edmund's eyes, and he held up his stick like a quarterstaff to fend them off.

He heard a strange choking sound behind him. From the corner of his eye, he saw Elspeth's torch fall to the ground, where it flickered out. Then she charged forward, the enchanted sword blazing in her right hand like all the light in the world.

With cries of terror, the thieves turned and fled, their footsteps thudding on the track long after they had been swallowed up by the shadows.

Edmund went over to Elspeth, who was staring at the sword as if she couldn't quite believe what she saw. The shimmering silver gauntlet and the crystal blade were fading, leaving only a faint glow around her hand.

'How did you do that?' he asked.

'I'm not sure,' she said, clenching and unclenching her hand as the last whisper of light vanished. 'It . . . it just appeared. I didn't know what to do with it.' She gave a small, nervous laugh. 'It's lucky the thieves didn't know that!'

'You should learn to fight with it properly,' Edmund told her. 'You might need to, if we're in as much danger as Aagard said.'

Elspeth looked down at her hand again and didn't reply.

'Awake and wandering in the moonlight, I see.' The voice came out of the dark and Edmund jumped. Cluaran was strolling towards them, his harp case on his back. The minstrel stopped when he saw his pack undone, its contents spilled out. 'What's this?' he demanded. 'Why have you disturbed my belongings?'

'We were attacked by thieves,' Edmund said. 'I needed a weapon.'

'You searched in vain, then,' the man said. 'My knife and bow travel with me always.' It sounded as if he didn't care they had been forced to fight for their lives, but then he beckoned them over to the fire and sat down with his legs crossed.

'You'd better tell me what happened,' he said. His gaze was as dark as the shadows around them when he looked as Elspeth. 'I want to know everything.'

Edmund told him about the attack, keeping the tale as brief as possible and saying nothing of his Ripente skills – nor of the sword. Aagard had warned him and Elspeth to trust only each other, and he saw no reason to tell Cluaran about the gifts that had been forced upon them since the storm. The minstrel listened without comment, only darting occasional glances at Elspeth while she sat in silence, absently rubbing her hand.

When Edmund had finished speaking, Cluaran looked at each of them sharply. 'So you saw them off, using nothing but a pair of torches?'

Edmund thought he heard mocking disbelief in the minstrel's tone. 'It was as I told you,' he snapped.

'And you, Elspeth?' Cluaran pressed. 'You're not hurt?'

Elspeth's restless fingers stilled and she looked up, shaking her head in a gesture that was half a shrug. Edmund willed her to say nothing about the sword. She met the minstrel's gaze and said, 'Yes. It was just as Edmund said.'

Cluaran stared into the fire. After a time he said, 'It seems to me that I should stay with you a while longer. You both have homes in the eastern kingdoms, you said? If you're planning to walk there across Dunmonia and Wessex, you'll need protection. You clearly have a way of attracting trouble.'

'We can manage very well alone,' Edmund said hotly, wishing for an instant that they *had* told the minstrel about the sword – the man's dismissal of them as helpless children was unbearable. 'We didn't need you tonight!' he pointed out.

'You were lucky, that's all. Do you want to trust to luck for the entire journey?'

'He's right,' Elspeth said unexpectedly. Edmund frowned at her, but she went on: 'Aagard made us promise to ask Cluaran for help, and he knows more about this journey than you do!'

Cluaran frowned. 'What exactly did Aagard make you promise?'

'That we would ask for your protection,' Elspeth said steadily. 'In the name of the one who never died.'

Cluaran leaped to his feet, his eyes blazing. He suddenly looked much taller, and Elspeth shrank back.

'He told you that?' he demanded.

She nodded, too frightened to speak.

'Do you know of whom he was speaking? Tell me truthfully.'

Elspeth shook her head. 'I do not,' she vowed.

'Nor I,' said Edmund.

Cluaran blinked and some of the rage faded from his gaze. Edmund wondered why it was so important to him that they should not have understood Aagard's words.

Abruptly, the minstrel turned away and walked to the other side of the fire.

'I already told you I would stay with you,' he said without looking at them. 'Aagard should not have demanded more.'

CHAPTER NINE

Elspeth looked up from the hare she was skinning and sighed, the sound swallowed up by the endless moor around her and the dull grey sky that stretched above. Her father had taught her to cook, but she was more familiar with fish than meat, and she was making a rough job of preparing the hare. She envied Edmund his skill at archery. Cluaran had insisted they work for their keep while they were with him, and the boy had proved so good with the bow that the minstrel had given him the job of providing food for the pot. Edmund was off now, stalking something for the next day. By comparison, cooking was dull work, but at least it kept Elspeth's hands busy, dulled the ominous prickling that still came and went in her right palm.

The sword had not appeared for three days now, but Elspeth knew it was always with her. Whenever she felt the minstrel's sharp eyes on her, she wondered if he suspected something. He had seemed doubtful they had needed nothing more than torches to drive off the thieves. Had he glimpsed the sword's brightness slicing through the shadows? If he had, why not say so? And who was the one who never died? Someone from Cluaran's past as well as Aagard's? So many questions she had, but the minstrel's reserve did not invite them to be asked.

Elspeth found Cluaran difficult to talk to about anything beyond the demands of their journey, but she did not share Edmund's deep mistrust of him. After that first night, the minstrel seemed to have accepted their company, speaking little but scrupulously sharing food and fire with them. *If he goes off on his own every night, that's his business*, Elspeth thought. At least he had led them unerringly so far, always knowing where to go if the path split or lost itself among rocks, knowing where to find water and wood.

A cry from a bird circling above her roused Elspeth from her thoughts, and she forced herself back to the task of skinning the hare. She worked slowly, and Cluaran had returned with water and made up the fire by the time she was finished.

'A fair job,' he pronounced, inspecting the carcass. 'You'll get better with time.' He showed her how to spit the animal over the fire, and left her to watch it while he fetched salt from his pack. The bundle was contrived to hold cookware, food, clothes and bedding in neat order. Elspeth was long used to stowing things well on board ship, and she marvelled at the supplies he had packed away: even the harp case had been put to use, with pouches for the bow and arrows along one side.

'It's foolish to sleep unarmed by the road in these times,'

Cluaran commented, following Elspeth's gaze. He looked at her levelly. 'As you well know. You were lucky those thieves didn't stay to cause real harm.'

Reddening, Elspeth turned back to the spit. 'We had the torches,' she muttered. 'And Edmund's a good fighter.'

'He has his skills,' the minstrel conceded.

Edmund came back with another brace of hares slung over his shoulder just as Cluaran pronounced the roast hare ready. They sat around the campfire, gnawing at the stringy meat while the last of the light faded. They spoke little. Elspeth was tired from the day's walking and Edmund was still subdued. But even he looked up with interest when Cluaran announced that they would reach a village before nightfall tomorrow.

'They know me there,' he told them. 'They'll give us a bed; but times are hard. These,' he gestured at Edmund's catch, 'will make us a deal more welcome.'

It would be good not to sleep on the ground for once, Elspeth thought, even if only for one night. She pulled her blanket more tightly around her, trying to make herself comfortable on the hard ground.

Edmund stirred, and turning towards him, she saw that his eyes were open. She began to speak to him, but he put a finger to his lips and jerked his head towards the other side of the fire.

Cluaran had risen noiselessly to his feet. Without a glance in their direction he turned and strode off into the darkness.

Elspeth waited until she judged the man must be out of earshot, but her voice was still hushed when she spoke.

'I wonder where he goes.'

Edmund shrugged. 'Who knows? Just be careful what you say – he walks so softly you can never hear his return.'

It is true, Elspeth thought, remembering the night of the attack when Cluaran had arrived seemingly out of nowhere. And not just Cluaran, but the thieves, too. She propped herself up on one elbow and frowned at Edmund.

'When those men attacked us, how did you know it was thieves coming, and not Cluaran?'

Edmund stared at her in silence for a long moment.

'I could see through their eyes,' he said at last.

'You mean ... you're Ripente!' Instinctively Elspeth drew back, her mind filled with stories of the second-sighted traitors who were bought by kings to spy upon their enemies.

'I may have their sight, but I am no traitor,' he spat back. Then he smiled bitterly. 'It took Aagard to recognise what I am, even if it is not what I wish to be. I didn't even know of it until the storm. Like you with the crystal sword.'

Elspeth looked down at her right hand, flexing the fingers. 'Then we both have a gift that's more of a curse.'

'But your sword saved us,' Edmund argued. 'All my gift has brought is trouble.' His face twisted with pain as he went on, 'Just before Aagard left us, do you remember what happened?'

'Aagard said his old enemy – Orgrim – tried to use your eyes. But you have the same power as he, don't you? And you fought him off.'

'I managed to push him away, that's all. But Aagard said he'd return, looking for the sword. And he knows me now, Elspeth!' Edmund turned away so she could hardly hear his next words: 'I don't know if I can keep him out next time.'

Elspeth felt a rush of sympathy. He sounded like a frightened boy, a long way from the powerful, shadowy Ripente figures who had been spoken of in hushed tones throughout her childhood. She longed to comfort him – and perhaps there was a way.

'I think you're wrong,' she said slowly. 'Orgrim has no reason to come back to you.' She winced when she saw Edmund's sudden hopeful look, and hoped she was right.

'Orgrim uses his power to spy, so how can he spy on someone who knows he's there?' she went on. 'Surely he'd look for someone who can't sense him in the first place?' She gulped. 'Someone like me,' she said with an effort. 'Perhaps I'm the one who needs to be prepared.'

Edmund's face was wary. 'What do you mean?'

'Could you look through *my* eyes?' Elspeth forced herself to ask.

'No!' he cried, twisting away.

'But think, Edmund!' she persisted. 'Aagard told us he had learned to feel when his eyes were being used. Maybe I can as well. The only way is if you try to use my eyes, so that

I recognise what it feels like. Otherwise, how will I ever know if Orgrim is trying to spy through me instead?'

Emotions chased across Edmund's face like clouds. 'You're right,' he said at last. 'But are you sure you want me to do this?'

Elspeth nodded with more determination than she felt. Edmund sat very still, concentrating his thoughts, while she braced herself, telling herself over and over that she had to trust Edmund, Ripente or no.

Nothing happened. Edmund's eyes were unfocused; his face as still as stone. After a moment Elspeth risked speaking.

'What did you see?'

He blinked and looked up, puzzled. 'I didn't. I couldn't see anything!'

'What do you mean?'

'I can't use your eyes,' he said. 'There's a sort of a . . . a whiteness around you.'

She stared at him. 'Has that ever happened before?'

'No!' He hesitated. 'But I've hardly used the power before. Perhaps I *can't* use it on everyone.'

'In that case,' she said with sudden hope, 'maybe Orgrim can't either!'

'Maybe not,' Edmund said. 'But it might be you.' He grinned. 'I don't think anyone could make you do something you didn't want to!'

Elspeth smiled back, but inside she doubted it had anything to do with her. How would a girl raised at sea be able to defend herself against the powers of a Ripente? It must be due to Edmund's inexperience. Orgrim had had years to master his art – and if he tried to see through her eyes, she was afraid she would betray all her secrets, and Edmund's, without ever knowing he was inside her mind.

Cluaran had returned by the time they woke. Wherever he had been, it had left him in a cheerful, busy mood.

'We've a long day's walk if we're to reach Akeham by night-fall,' he told them as they packed up their bedrolls.

The day was much the same as previous ones, following a twisting path through a wide, flat expanse of heath and bracken dotted with rocks. The minstrel strode ahead, occasionally humming or singing to himself, but making no effort at conversation; only sometimes turning to check they were still with him. By late morning, Elspeth found she needed most of her breath to keep up with him. But after last night's discussion of their unwanted gifts, she and Edmund were easier with each other, and they walked together companionably.

As the day wore on their path descended until they could see fields and woodland below them. The sun was low by the time they came to a little stream and followed it to a cluster of homes dwarfed by a great oak tree. The village was smaller than Medwel, the houses little more than straw huts. The chieftain's wife, a thin, mournful-looking woman, was milking her cow when they arrived. She clearly knew Cluaran and

did not look pleased to see him but, as the minstrel had pre-
dicted, she cheered up at the sight of the hares and agreed to
let the visitors sleep under her husband's roof. She penned the
cow in its byre behind the house and led them inside, telling
Cluaran to help her lift the planks off a storage pit in the middle of the floor.

'Reach in and pull me out the nearest sack,' she instructed.
The minstrel had to lie on the floor and stretch his arm down
into the darkness, and Elspeth guessed that whatever supplies
were kept there were running low. Eventually Cluaran pulled
up a half-full sack and the woman scooped two handfuls of
dried beans from it into her cooking-pot, measuring them out
with a careful eye.

The chief returned as Elspeth and Edmund were helping to
replace the last of the planks over the store hole. He was a
lanky, straw-haired man, as thin as his wife, with pale blue
eyes the colour of the sky at dawn. Cluaran looked small and
shabby beside him, his clothes patched and stained beside the
other man's thick woollen tunic. Yet the chief seemed nervous
around the minstrel, and made a point of offering him the
best seat near the fire. There were no stools for Elspeth and
Edmund, who had to sit on the wooden boards over the store
hole. Elspeth didn't mind being excluded from the circle of
conversation; she was too tired to talk, and the hut felt stuffy
after their last few nights in the open. Besides, sitting on the
rough planks felt oddly comforting, reminding her of her old
life on the *Spearwa*.

She was sharing an oatcake with Edmund, letting the buzz of fireside talk wash over her, when Cluaran held up his hand. It was nearly dark by now, and his thin face, lit on one side by the firelight, looked suddenly ominous.

'Listen,' he ordered.

Outside, there was a rapid, regular pattering sound. It became more distinct as they listened, and Edmund went pale.

'Horses,' he whispered.

Cluaran leaped to his feet. With a curt word to their hosts, he strode over and hauled Edmund upright as Elspeth, alarmed, jumped up too.

'Stand by the wall,' he told them, beginning to haul at the planks on which they had been sitting. The chief hurried to help him, and together they lifted three of the heavy boards, revealing a deep, dark space beneath.

'In there – both of you!' Cluaran ordered. As Edmund began to protest, he snapped, 'We've no time to argue! You must not be found here.'

The hoof beats were louder now. Elspeth peered into the dark store hole, wondering how deep it was.

'For gods' sake, girl, hurry!' said the village chief.

Behind him, his wife was wringing her hands. 'What have you brought on us?' she wailed to Cluaran. 'They'll kill us all if we're harbouring fugitives.'

Too frightened to speak, Elspeth dropped into the blackness. She landed on a pile of hay. Edmund shot down so fast beside her, she wondered if he had been pushed.

Cluaran's face appeared in the square of light above them. 'Not a sound,' he warned. 'I'll come for you when they've gone.' There was a scraping noise as he dragged the planks into place, and the light vanished.

Elspeth crouched in the prickly hay, listening to the sounds above them. The woman's complaints were a high keening; her husband's voice an indistinct mutter.

Then they heard Cluaran, clear and sharp from just above them. 'Tell them that Cluaran the minstrel was your only visitor, but he headed south before nightfall. With luck they'll come after me.'

His tread was so light that they did not hear him go, but the heavy door swung open and then shut.

It was cold in the store hole, and Elspeth drew closer to Edmund. As her eyes grew used to the blackness, she made out crumbling earth walls, chilly hay beneath them with the food sack propped on a higher pile at one side, and above, a single, faint chink of light through the boards. It seemed only moments before the hoof beats stopped outside. Almost at once there was a loud pounding on the door. Elspeth let out a terrified squeak, and felt Edmund's hand reach for hers in the darkness and clasp it – though whether to comfort her or him, she could not tell.

She heard a harsh query followed by quick, frightened answers, but could make out no words. Then heavy footsteps sounded over their heads. Elspeth strained her ears as the man with the harsh voice came into the house.

'An old man, Aagard by name. He's tall, white-haired. Has he been this way?'

'Aagard the healer?' The chief sounded genuinely surprised. 'He lives many leagues away, down on the coast. They say he hardly ever leaves his cave. What would you want with him?'

'None of your business! Give us some food, and we'll be off. Maybe this minstrel of yours will know more.'

Elspeth froze as more footsteps banged above them. Who were these men, and why did they want Aagard? And what would happen if they found her and Edmund instead?

At that moment the men seemed more intent on eating than searching. 'Only milk?' she heard in tones of disgust. 'Give us ale, woman!'

Elspeth was cold and cramped, but she dared not stir a muscle in case she made a noise that was heard in the room above. Instead, she kept still and listened to the boards creak under the weight of the visitors. The men above had been cursing their host's food and boasting of their horses, but now their conversation had taken a new turn. It made her flesh prickle and she felt Edmund tense beside her.

'Turned the cave upside down, and no sign of him or the sword. All we found was that empty sea chest. His lordship won't be pleased.'

'But we searched the coast for three leagues each way,' said the second voice. 'Could we have missed him at Medwel?'

'Where would he have hidden? There's barely a hut left standing!' The first man began to laugh. 'Did you see them run?'

The second man laughed too. Beneath their feet, Elspeth stared in horror at her hand. It was because of her sword that these men had murdered the people of Medwel, and meant to kill Aagard! Elspeth felt Edmund shaking – she did not know if it was with fear or fury.

At last an order was given, and there was scraping and clattering as the men got to their feet. Boots tramped across the boards once more, and – finally – there was the sound of hoofs outside, riding off.

Elspeth was too frightened to move, or suggest to Edmund that they climb out of their hiding place. Instead she sat, clasping his hand in hers, as the hay-scented darkness pressed around them.

CHAPTER TEN

Edmund dreamed he was in Gaul.

The *Spearwa* had just docked, and men and women lined the harbour to welcome her. Edmund gazed eagerly along the row of faces and, yes, there was his uncle Aelfred, tall as a tree. It was five years since Edmund had seen him, but there he was waving, with the teasing smile Edmund remembered so well. He had made his fortune, just as he'd vowed; behind him were the six black horses that he'd boasted he would buy, and his velvet cloak was fastened with a silver bird like Edmund's own, a gift from Heored for Aelfred's good service to Edmund and his mother during the king's many absences.

But soon there was something wrong. Aelfred's smiling face was swallowed up by people crowding forwards. The sky darkened and the harbour vanished behind towering waves, and Edmund was back in the storm, his ears filled with the groan of tortured wood, the shouts of terrified men, and overhead, something huge and dark, waiting for him.

He woke to utter blackness and the sound of quarrelling

voices. For a moment he floundered, lost and blind – then last night flooded back to him: the village of straw huts; the store hole; the men who had sat over his head and laughed about murder. Edmund's heart pounded and he strained to hear the speakers above his head.

'I told you we couldn't trust the half-stolen!' It was a woman's voice, the chief's wife.

What did she mean? Edmund wondered. He hesitated for barely a heartbeat before reaching out to look through her eyes. Daylight spilled through the open door and the chief, red-faced, was arguing back. There was no one else in the room.

Edmund blinked and brought back his sight. He reached for Elspeth and shook her by the shoulder. 'The horsemen have gone,' he said. 'We can get out, come on!'

They clambered stiffly to their feet, but the boards were too high to reach. They began to yell. 'Hello! Let us out of here!'

Light poured in as the planks were abruptly drawn back. Cluaran looked down on them, his face tight with anger.

'Cluaran!' Edmund was astonished. 'But you weren't –' He stopped – in three words, he had almost given himself away. 'I didn't hear you up there,' he corrected himself.

'And if one of those men had stayed here, you'd be in chains now.' The minstrel's voice was very cold. 'You were crowing louder than the village cockerel. I may be able to shield you from your enemy's eyes, but not from your own stupidity.'

He leaned over the edge of the hole to pull them up.

Edmund, his face flaming, took the minstrel's hand and let himself be hoisted into the room. Next Cluaran hauled up Elspeth. Their hosts watched nervously, standing very close together as if they were as scared of the minstrel and his travelling companions as they had been of the horsemen last night.

'We'll be on our way,' Cluaran told them.

The chief could hardly conceal his relief. 'Gods speed you on your journey,' he muttered, barely looking at Cluaran, while his wife, sour-faced, said nothing at all.

Cluaran walked them hard all morning – turning north, Edmund noticed, and only speaking to point out some hazard on the path. He did not even stop to eat at midday, but pulled a loaf from his pack and handed them chunks as they trudged on.

Edmund deliberately lagged behind to talk to Elspeth. 'You heard what those men were saying last night?' he murmured. 'About looking for the sea chest?'

She nodded. 'It's all because of this cursed sword,' she said bitterly. 'That's why they're hunting Aagard. Those poor people in Medwel.'

Edmund's mind shied away from the thought of the burning village. He could do nothing for those people, not now.

'Elspeth, if they're still looking for the sword, does that mean they are looking for us as well?'

'They didn't mention either of us. They can't know I have the sword.'

'Not yet,' he agreed. 'But Orgrim doesn't need soldiers to track people down. Once he knows you have the sword, he'll be able to send his men straight to us.'

'Do you think he can use his power on me, then? Even though you couldn't?'

'No.' Edmund spoke carefully. 'I think the sword protects you in some way, as Aagard suggested. But that doesn't stop you being in danger!'

'What do you mean?' Elspeth's voice was tense.

Edmund did not answer at once. *Orgrim knows me now,* he thought. *He could find me easily if he wanted to.* Were Ripente drawn to each other, somehow? He wished he had asked Aagard more when he had the chance, instead of being determined to know nothing about this unlooked-for gift!

All his life his father had been away on some campaign or other. Edmund's mother, Branwen, had mostly raised him alone, teaching him the management of a household and the behaviour fitting to a young prince. Branwen's brother, Aelfred, had been there for a time, and given Edmund his first lessons in swordsmanship and other courtly skills that his uncle hadn't thought him too young to learn. Edmund had been flattered to have the attention. He had few other true friends and, older though he was, Aelfred always seemed to know exactly how Edmund felt. Nightmares were soothed with magical tales; worries teased out. But then Aelfred too had gone away, to buy six black horses in Gaul, leaving Edmund to learn his duties from his mother once more, in readiness for the time when he would rule his father's kingdom.

Edmund's blood ran cold. Could a Ripente become a king? Or would he have to keep this skill secret from everyone, to protect his inheritance? More importantly, what danger was he bringing home with him?

He looked up to find Elspeth watching him. 'Orgrim could still reach you through me,' he told her. 'I don't know if I can push him away another time. You would be safer without me.'

Elspeth shook her head. 'No,' she said firmly. 'We should stay together. I know he's looking for me – well, for the sword. But splitting up won't keep either of us safe. And who knows, perhaps this enchantment will wear off. The sword will find another hand when it sees how useless mine is for wielding it!' She gave him a bitter smile, then nodded towards Cluaran's rapidly disappearing back. 'Besides, we have to stay together or risk losing the use of our tongues. After all, who else do we have to talk to?'

Cluaran slowed his pace as the sun started to curve down towards the horizon. The land around them was greener now, touched with early signs of spring, and when their path led them into woodland the minstrel stopped and waited for them to catch him up.

'Where are you taking us?' Edmund asked. 'Lord Gilbert said you were headed east, to Wareham.'

'I've changed my plans since then,' said Cluaran. 'We're going north to Glastening. I have business there.'

'There's a church in Glastening, isn't there?' Elspeth said. 'My father told me once.' She trailed off, her eyes darkening with pain.

They were walking through oak and beech trees, their branches still in bud, alongside a small stream. Cluaran seemed to have lost his earlier ill-humour; he was humming under his breath, as if their surroundings had cheered his spirits.

He led them through a gap in the trees and stopped. 'We've made good time,' he said. 'We will rest here awhile.'

Edmund looked past him and gasped. In front of them was a lake, not large but perfectly still. The water was a pure, clear green. The trees came down to the water in a horseshoe shape, trailing their branches on the shiny surface, sliced through with shafts of pale sunlight. A few early dragonflies flitted over the surface, but there was no other movement.

They sat down by the water. Elspeth sighed and leaned back, and Edmund felt some of his anxiety ebb away.

'This is the edge of the kingdom of Wessex,' Cluaran told them. 'We'll not enter the kingdom by the road. We'll need to tread warily from now on.'

Edmund looked at the minstrel with renewed suspicion. Why was he so sure that the horsemen were coming for them? He had hidden them in the chieftain's grain store as if he knew they were in danger all along. He clearly did not fear for himself, or he would have hidden too.

'Who were those men at the house last night, Cluaran?' Elspeth asked suddenly, echoing Edmund's thoughts so closely that he jumped.

The minstrel frowned. 'They are men of Wessex, known as the Guardians of the Realm. They travel as the king's men, but they do not serve him. Instead they are in the pay of a lord at King Beotrich's court, one of the King's Rede.'

'Orgrim!' murmured Edmund.

Cluaran gave them an odd look. 'Aagard has told you more than I thought.' His eyes narrowed, exaggerating his pointed features. 'Orgrim is an ambitious and cunning man,' he said, 'and the king's most trusted counsellor. He set up the Guardians with Beotrich's agreement, claiming that times had become so lawless that an extra force was needed. They go armed with swords, and are known throughout Wessex by the silver boss on their shields – known and feared.'

'But we weren't in Wessex last night,' Elspeth protested.

'It's Orgrim's purposes they serve, not the king's. Orgrim is persistent, and his reach is long.'

Edmund shuddered. 'But what does he *want*?'

'Power.' Cluaran's voice was quiet, and Edmund had to strain to hear. 'More power than he has now, more than you could ever imagine.' He stared at the lake for a moment, his face set like stone. 'If he is sending his men out of the kingdom, he must be close to achieving his goal, of holding more power in his hands than any mortal man before him. Aagard has sworn to stop him. And for my own reasons, so must I.'

'And that's reason enough for us to trust you?' Edmund challenged.

Cluaran raised one eyebrow. 'Trust me? I'm not asking for that. I have my own ends, which are nothing to do with you.' He gave them a brief, cold smile, but when his gaze rested on Elspeth, there was something else there, close to confusion and even fear. 'Aagard has bound me to protect you so I'll stay with you for now, and I'll keep you safe from Orgrim as long as you don't walk into his hands by yourselves. That's all.'

Edmund opened his mouth to retort, then stopped. Something had changed in the air around them. He stiffened – was someone listening? There was no sound apart from the minstrel's quiet voice and the lapping of the water. He sent his sight out a little way to search; it was becoming easier to do this each time, although still the thought of what he was doing made him queasy. There was no one around.

But –

Without warning, the intruder was in his head again. Panic shot through him. He recognised it instantly: the foggy miasma stretching itself into the corners of his mind, and at its heart the cold, metallic sense of purpose.

Try to close your mind, Aagard had said. Edmund strained to find the source. For an instant he stood on the edge of the chasm in his mind, fog pouring around him like smoke, before he leaned forward and pulled the edges closed. He felt a flash of fury, then nothing.

Trembling, he opened his eyes. His companions were looking at him; Elspeth with concern, Cluaran with sharp interest. But before either of them could speak, a new sound came to them, a distant drum of hoofs.

It's too late, Edmund thought in terror. *He's sent them back for us!*

'It's not the Guardians,' Cluaran said calmly. 'Wrong direction. But still –'

He gestured behind them to where the trees were thickest, and picked up a fallen branch to wipe their footprints from the muddy shore. Edmund staggered to his feet and followed Elspeth, who had snatched up their packs as she darted for the trees. Cluaran joined them a moment later, and led them further into the undergrowth.

Branches whipped Edmund's face at every step. Elspeth seemed to move as clumsily as he did, but Cluaran slipped between the thorns with ease. Before long he stopped, a finger to his lips, and gestured to them to crawl into a thicket of bramble. The spikes tore at Edmund's clothes, but he hardly felt them. The ragged thunder of the horses was drawing closer, drowning out even the thudding of his heart.

The hoof beats seemed to stop just yards away, though by their muffled sound Edmund guessed they were on the softer ground beyond the lake. A gruff voice shouted an order, and he heard men dismounting.

'Right, this is as far as we go. Let the horses drink and fill your bottles.'

'We're not going on, sir?'

'We're outside the king's realm already. The Guardians might go further, but our duty's in Wessex.'

There was the sound of splashing as horses were led into the water. Two of the men had wandered into the woods; their voices carried clearly to Edmund.

'I can't believe we've been sent all this way after an old man! What's this one done, d'you think?'

'Hah! Not paid his dues to the Guardians, like as not. Or looked squint-eyed at Lord Org—'

The other man shushed his companion as a third set of footsteps came up to them. A moment later the gruff-voiced captain spoke.

'Is there a problem with your orders, Tib?'

'No, sir!' said the man.

'Good. I'll have no disrespect here. We may not be Guardians, but we can still do our duty by King Beotrich and his Rede.'

As Tib stammered an apology, new hoof beats came cantering through the trees. To Edmund's ear the sound was sharper than before, in a way that made his skin prickle. He heard a gasp from one of the men, then a frantic scrambling to attention as the horseman approached.

'Captain Cathbar?'

There was a ring of something familiar in the voice, but

it was not the voice that froze him. The presence of the man beyond the trees hit Edmund like a wave. This was the force that had tried to possess him twice before; that he had only just shut out; that had howled at him with such malice.

Orgrim.

Keep him out! Edmund thought desperately. He pressed his face into the hard-packed ground, squeezing his eyes closed and throwing his arms over his head. He could feel the cold tendrils of thought reaching for him; frantically, he tried to shut his mind, lying still as a fox who hears the hounds scratching outside the earth.

'I have new orders for you, Cathbar. The old man is accompanied by two others. A youth, pale of skin and hair, blue-eyed, small in build. He is more powerful than he appears. And a girl, also young, a little taller. Black hair, amber eyes. Treat her with caution too; she may be a witch.'

Captain Cathbar's reply was so muted that Edmund could not make out the words. But the cold, refined voice of the Ripente was as clear as before.

'They are certainly near this place. Your orders, captain, are to find them and deliver them with all speed directly to the Guardians. I wish to question these traitors *myself*. Do you understand?'

The captain muttered an assent.

'And, Cathbar – I must make one thing quite clear. In the past, I believe, you have had some sympathy with the old man; even fondness for him, perhaps? But that was long ago. Now he is a traitor to his own king. I hardly need to tell you the penalty for aiding a traitor, captain.'

The captain did not reply. There was a scuffling as the men came to attention again, then another sharp clatter of hoofs as the Ripente rode off.

At the same moment, Edmund heard the beating of wings. As the hoof beats faded, he looked up to see a great black bird soaring away from them over the trees.

There was a brief, heavy silence.

'Looks like we're here for a while longer, then,' came Cathbar's voice.

He began to give orders to groups of the men; some to return to the road, others to start beating the woodland fringes. *We should run!* Edmund thought desperately. But then he realised that Cluaran was whispering to himself. He tried to signal to the minstrel to be quiet. Had he not heard that the men were coming for them?

The air grew cold. On the ground around them, the dust stirred. The wind began to rise as Edmund watched, and the dust with it, blowing over the bushes towards the lake. Next moment, the branches above them were rattling, the air full of whirling leaves. From the shore of the lake he could hear the horses stamping uneasily and the sharp calls of the men; one trying to calm his mount, another crying that he was blinded by dirt. The cries grew louder as the gale rose, sweeping up twigs to dance head-high.

Cluaran tugged at his arm, and Edmund jerked upright. As the wind became a howl, the three of them wriggled out from their hiding place, grabbed their packs and fled into the forest.

The captain's voice rang out behind them: 'I said stand *still*, you lackwits!'

They forced their way on, careless of the thorns and the whipping branches. Then even the shouts faded. The wind shrunk to a steady moan, and the first fat drops of rain plummeted through the leaves. They ran on, through taller trees now, and easier going, while the storm drummed and hammered over their heads.

It was late into the night before they rested. Fear had kept both Edmund and Elspeth on their feet, and Cluaran seemed to be able to find his way as well by dusk as by day. Eventually exhaustion made them stumble over every root and twig in their path, and Cluaran looked around for a place to stop. He found them shelter in the hollow of a giant yew, its foliage thick enough to shelter them as the storm blew itself out.

Elspeth sank gratefully on to the carpet of needles beside Edmund. When that cold-voiced man had spoken, she was sure Edmund had recognised him – she had seen him stiffen. And in the same instant she had felt the weight of the sword hilt in her hand. It had grown heavier and more distinct as the man spoke and, by the time the raven had flown down to him, she could see the gauntlet emerging from her skin and the faint edge of the blade shimmering through the brambles. What did it mean? The sword had faded as they ran through the wood, but her hand still tingled with it.

But she could not ask Edmund about any of this while Cluaran was listening. She turned to the minstrel instead.

'So where do we go now?'

'I have told you,' he said, stretching out on the damp ground as if it were a bed. 'We are heading for Glastening. We are in Wessex now, and there is danger everywhere. Stay on the road and we'll meet with soldiers. Be caught off the main highway and we'll be hanged as thieves. Glastening holds no more danger than anywhere else, and I have business there that I cannot now put off.'

CHAPTER ELEVEN

Glastening was bigger than any town Elspeth had visited before. The three travellers paused at the edge of the forest and looked down on the settlement. Below them were neat wooden houses surrounded by well-tilled farmland, and in the centre of the houses was a stone church with market stalls set up in front of it. Elspeth was eager to reach the town now. At least they would not stand out as much as they had done at the thane's house and at the place where they had hidden in the store pit. Cluaran had made sure of that.

He had left them in the shelter of the trees that morning and returned later with a bundle under his arm. 'These should fit you,' he'd said to Elspeth, holding out a boy's woollen tunic and leggings. 'The Guardians are looking for a boy and a girl. Let's show them two boys instead. We must cut your hair,' he added, pulling his knife from his belt. 'Edmund, this is for you.' He took out a little bottle that looked black in the trees' shadow. 'Walnut juice,' he explained, 'to dye your face and hair. You heard the soldiers – they are looking for a pale-haired boy and a girl with long dark hair. Well, they'll not find any such in this town while we are here.'

The boy's clothes felt strange to Elspeth, but they fitted well enough. She tried a nautical swagger as she strode down the hill towards the town. She saw Edmund laughing, and grinned back. It was the first time she had seen him really smile. His eyes looked light as water on his darkened cheeks and beneath his new peat-brown hair.

'You could be a peddler,' she joked, and then, when she saw Cluaran was not near enough to hear, she added, 'What would your parents think if they could see you now?'

'I think my father would disown me,' Edmund replied, his eyes dancing.

Cluaran came over. 'While we're at Glastening, you two are my apprentices,' he told them. 'We may stay a day or two, so be sure you do everything I say. I'll get us horses for the rest of the journey. There's still a fair way to go to Venta Bulgarum.'

Elspeth stopped walking. 'To Venta?' she echoed. 'But that's where Orgrim lives.'

'I never said you would enter the town with me.' Cluaran's voice was calm. 'I'll find you somewhere to hide outside while I conduct my business.'

The busy streets of Glastening were daunting after the quiet moors. Elspeth's eyes widened at the stone church tower that dominated the market square, and the crowds of people milling outside it. Brown-robed monks with shaven pates slipped through the crowd like dark-scaled fish, sometimes pausing to exchange a word with a tradesman in a leather jerkin, or a woman clad in fine-spun coloured tunic. Elspeth was so busy gawping at a woman's amber necklace that she collided with a boy who was staggering under a woven hamper. The basket squawked wildly and as she dodged the cloud of feathers that pursued her, she almost fell under the wheel of a passing cart.

Cluaran hauled her clear and gave her a hard look.

Just then a bell rang out, and for a moment the din quietened. The crowd thinned as monks and some of the townspeople left their business and streamed towards the church. Soon the sound of men's voices came from within, raised in a chant.

Elspeth's eyes filled with tears. 'Evensong,' she breathed. She remembered the nights between voyages when her father had taken her to pray for calm seas. '*Father!*' she murmured, and without a second thought, she ran to the great doors of the church and slipped into the candle-lit shadows.

The market people were closing their stalls when the service ended and they came back out into the fading afternoon light. Edmund had followed Elspeth into the church and sat beside her on a bench near the back. He had understood little of the Latin words and found the candles and the darkness oppressive, but it was a relief to be out of the market noise and away from Cluaran's orders. From the corner of his eye he had studied Elspeth's devotions. She had joined in all the prayers, murmuring along to the monks' chants. She clearly knew them as well as he knew the rituals of his mother's household gods.

Cluaran met them as they came out, accompanied by a stout monk whom he introduced as Brother Anselm.

'He's cellarer for the monks – in charge of food and supplies,' he told them. To the monk he said, 'Anselm, these are the two apprentices I told you of. Well-meaning lads, though slow at times.'

'I see they're good Christian boys, at least,' the monk said approvingly. Edmund blinked. He must have looked more at home in the church than he had felt. 'You must be our guest for supper tonight,' the monk continued, addressing Cluaran. 'The abbot will be pleased if you'll sing a saint's life for us. Such skill you have with the holy songs, it's hard to believe you're not of the true faith.'

Cluaran shook his head with a half-smile.

'And your lads?' said Brother Anselm. 'Can they hold a tune as well as you?'

'Alas, no,' Cluaran said. 'They've little skill, either of them. But they'll help you in the kitchen and wait at table tonight, if you tell them their duties. Elis here,' he gestured towards Elspeth, 'is simple-minded; he'll not talk much.' He glanced meaningfully at her. 'But he can cook, so set him to watch the spit. The other boy, Ned, can split logs and move a cask, for all his puny looks.'

Edmund opened his mouth to protest, but the minstrel turned on his heel, leaving them in the charge of Brother Anselm.

Elspeth's glare of indignation matched Edmund's, but then she shrugged, raising a finger to her lips to warn him to keep silent. The monk led them to a cluster of buildings behind the church, and took them into the stone-walled hut that contained the kitchen. Hams and onions hung from the blackened beams. Anselm set them to chopping vegetables on a block while he went off to stir the great central fire.

'Does Cluaran think we're his slaves?' Edmund hissed when he saw the monk busy with poker and bellows.

Elspeth chopped savagely at a carrot. 'He's sent us here to keep us out of the way,' she muttered. 'He doesn't even trust us to keep our mouths shut. Simple-minded indeed!' She split a turnip with one blow.

Edmund set to chopping a string of small shiny-skinned onions. But when he looked up again, his eyes stung with fumes, he could have sworn he saw a smile on Elspeth's lips, and he wondered what she was planning.

The monks' refectory was in a great hall, far bigger than the kitchen. With the crowd of monks, novices and guests at supper, it soon grew hot and steamy. Edmund and Elspeth were called hither and thither, bearing pitchers of ale and carrying bread to the four long tables, while Brother Anselm and his kitchen novices served soup and meat. Cluaran, who was sitting at the guests' table between an aged pilgrim and a puffed-up merchant with a silver chain, ignored them totally.

Edmund was fetching more ale at the great cask when he saw Elspeth pass by with a charger piled up with flat loaves. She began to set the bread down at intervals along the table, leaning between the guests who went on eating and talking as if she was not there. As she approached Cluaran she paused, then seemed to trip, tilting her charger and sending the bread tumbling over the table. A loaf splashed into Cluaran's soup, and another in his lap. The minstrel sat very still and didn't look up. Edmund choked, caught between laughter and horror – *don't draw attention to us!* With relief, he saw that no one else had noticed. As Elspeth passed him with the empty bread board, she gave him a sly wink.

Servants are invisible! Edmund thought. He should have known that from his own court. Cluaran had chosen their disguises well, for all their indignation.

'You've worked hard enough tonight, lads!' said Brother Anselm, waving them both from the room. 'Leave off now and take your own meal in the kitchen.'

At the end of the evening, Cluaran sang the tale of 'Saint Erkenwald'. Edmund sat on a heap of rushes just outside the hall doorway to listen. The minstrel's sweet voice rang, clear as birdcall. When the song ended there was tumultuous applause, and calls for more. Cluaran sang again, this time in the strange language Edmund had heard before. There was meaning enough in the sound – conflict and love and jealousy and longing – but not in the words themselves.

When the monks filed out of the dining hall and into the church for their night-time service, Edmund saw Cluaran stay behind to speak with three of the other guests, hard-faced men in dark cloaks who scowled at his approach. But they still withdrew into a corner with the minstrel to talk in low voices. Edmund watched them from inside the door, wondering what Cluaran was up to, until a young monk shooed him away, saying that he and Elis were to sleep in the stables behind the abbot's house. Cluaran did not look up as they left.

Next morning, the minstrel seemed distracted as he led them to the market square. He stopped outside the church and pulled a small clinking pouch from inside his tunic. Shaking the contents on to his palm, he handed Edmund and Elspeth a few copper coins.

'You can buy food in the market,' he told them, nodding towards the far side where early-arriving traders were already setting up stalls.

'Market day was yesterday,' said Elspeth in surprise. 'How can there be one today?'

'It's the spring festival,' Cluaran explained. 'It lasts for three days – even when there's no spring to speak of.' His face was faintly mocking; the sky above was cold and grey with clouds. 'But that's a mark of all the children of Adam: they drink and laugh for the entertainment's sake. And it's as well for me,' he added in a lighter tone. 'I've a living to earn, after all.'

More people were in the square now. Looking away down the road, Elspeth could see carts rolling into the town, and a man walked past leading a string of horses.

'Meet me back here at sunset,' Cluaran told Elspeth and Edmund. 'And do not draw attention to yourselves.' He turned and walked briskly after the horse trader.

As the square became busier, Edmund saw that Cluaran was right; this was as much a fair as a market, with peddlers selling amulets and strings of beads and good-luck charms, and entertainments set up among the food stalls. A ragged man was playing the bagpipes for flung coins, and one or two booths offered fortune-telling or games of chance. Edmund felt a giddy sense of freedom as they wandered among the early buyers; he could not walk like this at home without some guard dogging every footstep.

When they grew hungry, their noses led them to an open hearth where a whole pig was spit-roasting over a charcoal fire. Soon they were sinking their teeth in chunks of meat, the fat dribbling down their chins.

By mid-afternoon, more entertainers had arrived – pipers, singers, a stout boy with a big drum.

'Find the ball, sirs, find the ball! You, my lady, care to try your luck? A silver piece if you can uncover it.'

The ringing cry made Edmund stop by a booth draped in fabric the colour of ox blood. A small crowd had gathered round the table where a burly man brandished three cups, tossing them in the air one at a time before upending each on a board. Then he held up a painted wooden ball and placed it under the middle cup with a flourish.

'I've seen this trick,' Elspeth whispered as the man began to move the cups rapidly over the board. 'It looks easy, but you can never find the ball.'

First one and then another customer paid his penny and made his guess, but it seemed that the stall owner could not be beaten. His hands were huge, almost hiding the little cups, yet they moved with dizzying speed, flicking the cups in complicated patterns without ever lifting one from the table. Edmund saw that Elspeth was watching the progress of the cups with growing fascination.

'It must be that one!' she muttered, staring at the left-hand cup as the hands stopped moving. The latest customer thought so too; he pointed to the cup on the left.

'It's not there,' murmured Edmund, shaking his head. 'He's moved it back to the right again.'

With a flourish, the man raised the left-hand cup to show that it was empty. 'And here it is!' he boomed, producing the yellow-painted ball from the right-hand cup as the customer marched off, leaving behind his copper coin.

Elspeth turned to Edmund, open-mouthed. 'You saw him switch it! Or,' she added quietly, 'did you use . . . you know . . . ?'

'I don't think so,' Edmund said. 'Or maybe I did, without

realising.' He flushed guiltily – it felt like cheating – but all the same, why not? He concentrated on the stallholder. There was a moment of uncertainty, then he found himself looking from the man's own viewpoint. He could see the table beneath him, the great hands flashing to and fro. He could not see what the wooden ball was doing. But somehow he knew where it was. It was as if the man was focusing with more intensity on the cup that held the ball.

He felt something else, too: a flicker of thought that sent him back to himself in a rush. The man despised his audience. He saw them all as fools, to be played with and duped.

Three more customers tried their luck and failed. Each time, Edmund whispered to Elspeth: 'The middle one.' 'Now the right again,' – and each time, he was right.

'You should play him yourself!' Elspeth said. 'I have a coin left.'

Edmund thought for a moment. The man was so contemptuous, he deserved to be shown he was not dealing with fools after all. He nodded, took the coin from Elspeth and stepped forward to lay it on the table.

'Trying your luck, young man?' asked the stall owner, already moving the cups about. At first Edmund tried to concentrate on the movement, but he knew he didn't need to. Looking through the stallholder's eyes, it was obvious where the ball was each time.

'The cup on the left,' he said when the showman's hands stopped moving.

The man's face stiffened. 'Are you sure now?' His voice was cheerful, but his eyes had narrowed. When Edmund nodded, he lifted the cup. The ball rolled out – and a shout of approval went up from the watchers. Edmund held out his hand for the prize, but the stall owner, beaming around at his audience, raised his hand for silence.

'You've a keen eye, I see,' he said, looking at Edmund. 'And you're game for a wager, I'll be bound!' He picked out a small stack of coins from his leather bag, holding them between finger and thumb. 'Ten silver coins if you can find the ball twice more! What do you say?'

Don't draw attention to yourselves, Edmund remembered too late. The audience had swelled to a small crowd, drawn by the cup-and-ball man's ringing voice. In the front, Elspeth watched bright-eyed.

'Go on, Edmund!' she urged.

From all around, people shouted conflicting advice.

'Take your money, boy; don't be a fool!'

'Peace, woman, can't you see the luck is with him? Go for the purse, lad!'

Edmund hardly heard any of them. It had been hard taking coppers from Cluaran for today's food; at home, Edmund had handed out silver to his father's people without thinking twice.

'I'll wager,' he announced, to the delight of the crowd.

'Another coin, then, if you please,' said the showman, matter-of-factly.

Edmund faltered. 'But I don't have . . .' he began. The people nearest to him heard, and began to hoot their disappointment. He felt his face heating, but there was nothing he could say. Burning with embarrassment now, he started to turn away.

But the showman had scented a mark, and would not give up so easily. 'Come now,' he cut in. 'A well-set-up young man like yourself will have something about you that you can wager. A ring or a brooch perhaps?'

Before Edmund could move he stepped round his stall and twitched aside Edmund's cloak. Edmund angrily knocked his hand away, but not before the man's sharp eyes had spotted his name-brooch glinting in the muddy folds of his cloak. His meaty face crinkled in delight.

'There, you see?' he crowed. 'That silver birdie will do fine.' He was talking to the crowd now, over Edmund's head. 'And you can't back out of a wager, can you?' There was a mutter of agreement as people pressed forward, eager for the show.

Beside him, Edmund felt Elspeth tense. *We should run*, he thought. But a cold determination, hard as stone, had seized him. The showman meant to cheat him, but Edmund knew for sure that the man would fail. He pulled his cloak tight around him, hiding the brooch, and took a confident step towards the booth.

'I'll wager,' he said clearly.

'What are you doing?' hissed Elspeth.

Edmund had no time to explain. All his thoughts were fixed on the showman, who had gone back to the other side of his stall. Soon the huge hands were making the cups dance across the board. Edmund realised that this time he was not looking through the man's eyes, but focusing on the wooden ball itself – and it seemed the ball was answering him. He still knew where it was! Fierce triumph filled him as the hands skittered and whirled.

'The middle one,' he said, hardly looking at them.

He was right. The crowd roared.

Now the man was working in earnest. His face was set as he held up the ball and replaced it beneath the left-hand cup. Catching his mood, the crowd fell silent.

Once more Edmund followed the movement of the invisible ball: centre, to right, to centre again. Then, with no warning, it vanished.

Edmund wondered if anyone had heard his gasp. He had *felt* the ball there, under the cup. Now there was just a sense of emptiness. He heard the murmur of the crowd above the sound of the cups sliding on the table, and then caught sight of a sly glint in the showman's eyes. No, he had not lost his power. If he stretched his mind he could still feel the wooden ball – not on the table but somewhere else, hidden.

Edmund waited till the meaty hands had stopped moving. When he did not speak at once, the man raised his arms in a wide gesture.

'Take your time,' he said pleasantly, but Edmund could feel the malice beneath.

'The ball is not there.'

For a moment the two of them stared at each other, then the man broke into a hearty laugh.

'And how could that be, young sir? As all these good people can tell you, I haven't raised a cup from the table. No, I've carried out my side of the wager quite fairly!' His voice was jovial, but his gaze was stony. 'Choose a cup.'

Edmund groped with his mind for the little wooden sphere. There it was: low down, rolling in the grass. He turned to the watching crowd, who had started to mutter, siding with the showman.

'Look under the cups!' he said. 'You'll see he's lying. There's a hole in the table.'

Elspeth started forward, but before she could reach the table a stout, angry-faced woman whom Edmund recognised as one of the stall's earlier customers pushed her out of the way.

'Let me see those!' the woman bellowed, and before the showman could stop her she had knocked over all three cups. 'All empty!' she announced. 'I'll have my money back, thank you!'

As the man began to argue with her another townsman grabbed at the cloth hanging around the stall, ripping it away. The missing ball was clearly visible on the ground beneath the table. The people surged forward, yelling, and the showman took to his heels.

Elspeth grabbed Edmund's arm. 'We must leave, *now*,' she said, pulling him across the square.

'Yes, but not that way,' he told her. 'Let's hide in the church.'

But when they reached the church, the doors were shut. Edmund cursed and ran around the building, Elspeth close behind. He headed for the abbot's stables, and the empty stall where they had spent the night.

'We can wait here till sunset. It's not far off now,' he told Elspeth.

She nodded, her face unhappy. 'I'm sorry, I shouldn't have told you to try the game. Now everyone will remember us.'

'We were both stupid,' he said bitterly. 'I wanted the money, and I wanted to show I could beat him. But it was more than that.' In spite of himself, he felt a prickling of excitement at the memory. 'I *knew*, Elspeth. I knew where that ball would be, each time. This isn't the power Aagard said I had; it's something more. The ball doesn't have eyes! Nor a mind to read. This is beyond Ripente power. I have to find out what I can do with it.'

'Well, now,' said a familiar voice. 'There's some might say you done enough already.'

Elspeth spun round. The cup-and-ball man was standing in the stable yard behind them, his face mottled with fury.

'You lost me a tidy sum today,' he snarled. 'Not to mention giving away the tricks of the trade. So we'll start with you giving me that silver bird of yours.' He lunged towards Edmund.

Elspeth sprang forward, the sword scorching beneath her skin. But she stopped just in time. Sunlight glinted off a short, squat blade.

The man was holding a dagger to Edmund's throat.

CHAPTER TWELVE

I won't die like this, Edmund thought. *Not for such foolishness.* Shame burned in his chest and the fear vanished. He drove his foot hard into his assailant's shin. The man cursed and staggered, but kept one hand gripping Edmund's neck. Edmund slammed his elbow into folds of soft flesh, then felt a rush of savage satisfaction as the man grunted and pulled back. His grip slackened enough for Edmund to twist his head away, painfully shaving his chin as he tried to dodge the blade of the dagger.

Still gasping from the elbow jab, the showman grabbed Edmund in both arms like a bear. Edmund kicked out again and again, and managed to sink his teeth into a fleshy forearm. It stank of rancid fat, but the man flinched.

Edmund writhed like an eel, feeling his cloak tear. He ripped himself free and darted clear, leaving a square of cloth in his attacker's hand.

The man laughed softly. 'Lads, lads!' His voice was hoarse, his gaze still fixed on Edmund. 'There's no need to get yourselves hurt! Throw me the brooch, and the wager is settled.'

'Never,' said Edmund. 'You've not kept your side of the deal, so why should I keep mine?'

The showman's lip curled back. 'Because I am armed, and you are not?' he suggested with a sneer, taking a step towards him.

Edmund backed to the stable doors. He could hear horses shifting uneasily inside. When he felt the door's iron bolts jab in his spine, he stopped. The showman reached him in two strides and lashed out again, and this time the blade seared into Edmund's arm.

Through a mist of pain, he heard Elspeth shout – and the world exploded in white light.

Edmund threw up his unhurt arm against the dazzle. He heard the man's oath, the clang of metal, the whinnies of frightened horses.

When he could look through the glare, the showman was standing stock-still, staring at the hilt of his dagger. The blade had been sheared clean off. Beside him stood Elspeth, the crystal sword flaring in her silver-clad hand, filling the yard with pulsing light.

The man moved first. Still holding the useless hilt like a weapon, he took a step sideways, his red face the colour of clay.

'It's witchcraft you use, is it?' he snarled, his voice unsteady. 'I'll have the Guardians on to you!'

Elspeth said nothing, just stepped forward and brought the sword up over her head, ready to strike again.

The man's nerve broke. With a howl of terror, he threw down the knife hilt and ran from the yard.

For a long moment Elspeth stood with the sword raised over her head. Then she let out a long breath and let her arm fall.

The sword had come when she called it – and there had been a *rightness* to its appearance, as if the sword had answered her. Power had surged through her, a bolt of fire, with a shard of ice at its heart. *Nothing can hurt you*, it had promised, *nothing* . . .

'Your sword can cut through metal!' she heard Edmund exclaim.

Elspeth said nothing, just stared at her hand. The sword was beginning to fade, and her skin was visible through the silver gauntlet.

She shivered. The day had turned cold. The sun had dipped behind the stable buildings and the yard lay in deep shadow. In the gloom, Edmund's face loomed palely beneath the sweat-streaked walnut juice. His blue eyes held her like the bluest rock pools. Then Elspeth noticed the bloody gash along his chin, and saw the awkward way he held his arm as he picked up his torn cloak.

'You're hurt!' she cried. 'Let's go to the abbot's house. There will be a healer among the monks.'

'No time,' he snapped, and she could tell it took an effort for him to speak. 'We have to meet Cluaran. That man will have told the Guardians about us by now.'

Elspeth felt the weight of the sword vanish, the mesh of the gauntlet dissolve into her skin. 'We said we'd wait for Cluaran in the market,' she reminded him. 'We'll just have to hope he comes soon.'

Edmund nodded, his face strained. Praying he wouldn't faint, and draw even more attention upon them, Elspeth led the way back into the main square.

The stallholders still there were lighting torches, fixing them to poles beside their booths. Elspeth looked around anxiously, hoping against hope to spot Cluaran in the crowd. But the minstrel was nowhere to be seen.

'I think one of the stalls had medicines for sale,' she said. 'We could trade something.' But when she saw Edmund's face, she knew it was no good. He could not show his bleeding chin around the stalls for fear of attracting too many questions.

Edmund clearly had the same thought. He pulled up his hood. 'We can't risk showing ourselves,' he said. 'Maybe we should stay by the church.'

'But that's where they'll look for us first!' said Elspeth. 'We'll be safer in the crowd.' She caught Edmund's hand and dragged him into the throng, keeping her head bowed. Where was Cluaran? Had the minstrel got wind of the upset and taken off to save his own skin?

Torches now flickered and flared at every booth and stall. At opposite ends of the square, a fiddler and a bagpipe player sent out conflicting melodies, and in between, the queue at a pudding-woman's stall was being entertained by a boy juggling clubs.

Suddenly Edmund tugged her arm.

'What is it?'

He nodded towards the juggler. On the far side of the crowd, directly opposite them, was the cup-and-ball man. He was talking earnestly to a dark-dressed man with a sword hanging at his belt.

'Run!' Edmund hissed. Elspeth swung round to follow him into the crowd, but it was too late. The showman had spotted them.

'Hey!' he yelled. 'There! Over there!'

Elspeth sped after Edmund. He was heading for the church, instinctively seeking sanctuary with the God that was not his own.

But as they drew nearer, the great doors swung open, and instead of candlelight and monks' chanting, out spilled three armed horsemen, with more behind. The horses' hoofs clattered on the stone flags and torchlight danced on the shields' silver bosses.

The Guardians!

'Back to the market!' Edmund cried, spinning round.

They dived back among the stalls. Elspeth squirmed between fat bellies and bony elbows; earned foul curses and a slapped ear as she struggled to keep track of Edmund for, wounded though he was, he pressed ahead like a rabbit bolting through a warren.

Just as she caught up with him, there were cries of panic from behind, indignant yells and the jingle of spurs as the Guardians urged their horses through the crowd.

'Quick,' Elspeth hissed. 'This way!' She dived under the awning of an ale booth with Edmund on her heels. They watched the horses' legs clatter by, then dived under the next stall, and the next.

One of the horsemen yelled, 'The one with a wound on his chin can be spitted, but the other's to be kept alive!'

Elspeth shuddered. A faint, familiar pressure started in her right hand. *Not now!* she willed it fiercely. *Don't give us away!*

There was a crash as a booth was overturned behind them; cries of alarm as its torch caught the awning of the next-door stall. There was a gust of black smoke and people reeled away, shielding their eyes and mouths. Elspeth seized the chance to dash across the space to the next row of stalls. The blood pounded in her ears. Behind she could hear Edmund's laboured breathing.

Now they were on the edge of the square, peering into the shadows beyond the market lights. Nothing stirred in the blackness of the streets, but one wrong move and the horse-men would be upon them.

Then something moved in the darkness. 'He's here!' Edmund cried, running into the gloom.

A man was leading three horses towards them, not the sleek mounts of the Guardians but market horses, saddled and bridled.

It was Cluaran.

CHAPTER THIRTEEN

'You needn't think we've escaped,' Cluaran warned. 'The Guardians don't give up their quarry that easily.'

The minstrel's voice was like ice as he helped Elspeth to mount. His tongue clicked crossly when he heard Edmund's gasp of pain. Then he led them in silence, moving stealthily to the town gate. But once through the gate and out of earshot, he urged them into a gallop, as fast as their stocky little beasts could manage. Soon they were leaving the road and heading across open grassland.

Edmund's arm had begun to throb, but the pain mattered little compared to the relief of breaking free. He held the reins one-handed, sitting lightly in the battered leather saddle. All around the stars glowed brighter as his eyes grew used to the darkness.

Elspeth rode at his side. She clung awkwardly to the mare, her face grimly set, hands clutching the mane. The minstrel, though, rode as one born to it.

Edmund urged his horse alongside Cluaran's. 'Where are we going?'

'The Tor,' Cluaran snapped. 'We can lose the Guardians in the maze.' He spurred his horse faster, but Edmund reined his in to keep pace with Elspeth. He listened for signs of pursuit, but heard nothing beyond the dull thud of their own horses' hoofs. Edmund closed his eyes, sending his mind's sight back as far as he could towards Glastening.

There. He could see the head of a horse thundering over the ground, a fine beast, taller and sleeker than his own wretched nag. Other horses raced beside with dark-cloaked figures crouched over the reins. Soon they would gain on them, there was nowhere to hide . . .

Edmund wrenched his thoughts back and dug his heels into the flanks of his flagging beast.

Ahead of them, and blotting out the stars, loomed the hump-backed blackness of a tall hill. Lines scored the mound from side to side. As his pony's hoofs were muffled by a patch of long grass, Edmund heard hoof beats drumming on the road behind. The Guardians were closing on them.

Cluaran yanked at his horse's reins and turned on to a new track that headed sharply uphill. The track veered to the left and vanished between sheer walls of packed earth. Cluaran kept going, even though his horse laid back its ears and baulked at entering the narrow space. Elspeth's mare kept her nose close to the tail of Cluaran's horse and trotted after it, but Edmund, hanging back, had to spur his mount before the pony followed its companions.

The walls were higher than their horses' heads and formed

a narrow, roofless tunnel. Their hoof beats echoed like muffled drums, and Edmund forced himself to let his horse pick its way slowly over the earthen floor. The track curved steadily to the right, and he realised they must be inside the maze, winding their way up the sides of the Tor.

They had not ridden far when Cluaran halted his mount and said quietly, 'Stay close behind me. This is not a place to enter lightly – not a place for horses at all; but needs must.'

'Where are we?' Elspeth hissed, but the minstrel ignored her and led the way into the dark opening.

They had to go in single file. The sides of the maze closed in on them, the path barely wide enough for the little market ponies. Edmund felt a jolt of panic; *like being buried alive*, he thought, despite the narrow track of stars above. His feet kept brushing against the walls. Ahead of him, the tail of Elspeth's horse swished uneasily, but on and upwards they rode, the path always curving to the right until they seemed to be travelling in perfect circles.

'Elspeth?' he whispered.

But when she turned to him, her face a pale blur in the gloom, Cluaran hissed, 'Quiet!'

Another slow circuit of the hill, and Edmund sensed a vibration around him, first from the walls, then from the ground itself. His horse's ears flicked back. The Guardians had entered the maze. Ahead, Cluaran quickened his pace.

The vibrations grew to a steady rumble. Edmund could tell the men were gaining on them. He urged his horse faster along the dark and winding passage. On and on, with only the strip of star-flecked sky above to show they had not vanished far underground. Just when he thought he could bear no more, they rode under a stone arch and out in the fresh air, out under the wide black sky where he could breathe. He gulped down the cold night air.

'We're at the top,' Cluaran whispered. Ahead of them was a denser blackness against sky; too smooth and square to be hillside. Cluaran held up his hand for them to wait, then started forward as a half-moon rose above them and lit up the darkness.

They had emerged amid the ruins of an old temple. Its columns lay tumbled about on the stone floor, but on the furthest side a portico of slender marble pillars held up a carved stone slab against a sheer rock face. The hill fell away into blackness on either side, but as Cluaran led them through the fallen columns, Edmund saw a slab of thicker darkness between the standing pillars. Was it a doorway into the earth?

At their backs, the sound of hoofs rolled like thunder.

'Go!' Cluaran hissed, pointing through the pillars to the doorway. 'Now!'

Edmund fumbled with the reins, trying to coax his horse forward. It was wary, shying at shadows. When he dug in his heels, the beast lunged forward, almost unseating him.

'Hurry!' Cluaran cried.

Elspeth's horse pressed up behind, and at last Edmund was through the door. The stone portal seemed to glow with unearthly light, and for a moment Edmund did not know if he was seeing it with his mind or his eyes. The strange white gleam revealed that he was inside a stone chamber that fell away steeply to a dark tunnel. On every side of the chamber, the walls were carved from floor to roof with intricate lines and scratches. A web of runes? A shiver shot down Edmund's spine. What hand had left these marks in this gods-less place?

He turned to make sure Elspeth had followed, and saw the horsemen burst out from the tunnel beyond the temple ruins. Edmund froze as he heard the furious yells, saw moonlight glinting on drawn swords. Cluaran wheeled his horse around, yelling in a language Edmund did not know. In a single movement, the minstrel had his bow in hand, an arrow primed, but he did not fire.

Elspeth turned her horse and spurred it through the fallen columns, a white glow shooting from her right hand.

'Elspeth – no!' Edmund cried. She could not fight so many! But the light stabbed his eyes, brighter than ever before, and he was forced to close them, wincing. When he opened them again, Elspeth had reined her horse to a standstill between Cluaran and their pursuers. In her hand, the sword blazed like caught lightning.

The Guardians halted in confusion, their horses shying away from the glare. But Elspeth made no move to attack them. Instead she raised the crystal sword and aimed a blow at one of the pillars supporting the entrance to the cave.

The blade sheared the stone in two. Slowly, slowly, the portico tipped forward, taking the pillar top with it. Elspeth's horse leaped away from the tumbling stone. Elspeth and Cluaran charged into the chamber, barging Edmund out of the way. Over his shoulder he glimpsed the horror-struck face of a Guardian, his horse rearing in terror, as the great mass of stone crashed to the ground, sealing the doorway behind them.

Now they were in blackness, except for the fading glow of the crystal sword. The musty fug of damp earth and horse sweat filled Edmund's nostrils. The beasts pressed together in the narrow cavern, nervous and fretful.

Elspeth leaned against the neck of her mare, stroking the horse with her left hand and holding the sword away from her.

'Will she be all right?' she whispered to Edmund.

He nodded. 'She's just frightened,' he said. He could not keep his eyes from the sword, fading now, yet filling the cavern with an icy light. The blade had blurred to transparency and he could see the rock wall behind.

Cluaran spurred his horse alongside Elspeth's. He was staring at the sword as if he would look at it for ever. He put out a hand, but before he could touch the blade, he let it drop and turned his horse away, towards the tunnel at the back of the cave. His face was expressionless, but Edmund was sure the minstrel knew exactly what the sword was, just as Aagard had done.

'Follow close,' Cluaran told them. 'Elspeth between. Her mare is slower. Do *not* lose sight of me. You two should not be here, and the dwellers under the hill can be unforgiving.' Then he plunged into the tunnel, Elspeth following, and the darkness dropped like a sack over Edmund's head.

The horses' hoofs made almost no noise in the soft earth tunnel. Edmund found himself straining to catch the smallest sound. Sometimes he thought he could hear low-pitched voices chanting, and once the clang of iron on stone, but always so faint and distant that he could not be sure if it was only his imagination. He could tell that the path was descending, but he had lost all sense of direction, and of time too. Whenever a sudden draught of air indicated the presence of a side passage, Cluaran would urge his horse faster, hissing an order over his shoulder to stay close behind. Edmund wondered what was to be found down those side tunnels. *Better not to know*, he told himself uneasily.

After a while – he could not tell how long – he sensed a lessening of pressure in the air around him, and began to smell fresh earth again. There was a small lifting of the darkness too; he realised he could see the dim shape of the horse in front of him.

'We wait here,' Cluaran said, reining his horse to a halt. 'Make no sound.'

They waited, unmoving, for what seemed like an age. Edmund strained his ears, but could hear nothing beyond the horses' breathing. The grey light increased till he could see the smooth stone wall beside him. There were more carvings on it – some kind of symbols: people, birds, insects? Edmund leaned towards the wall for a closer look – but then the minstrel stirred.

'The Guardians are in the lowest level of the maze,' he said quietly. 'They'll head back to the opening and wait there for us to come out. We must go softly.'

As Cluaran led them forward, Edmund felt a fresh breeze on his face, and moments later he blinked in the milky light of early dawn. They were on the furthest side of the hill now, perhaps several leagues away from the maze entrance. All the same, Cluaran bid them be quiet, saying there was little cover ahead, and they must go slowly so as not to excite attention.

Tussocky grassland stretched all around them and Edmund's fingers twitched on the reins with the urge to gallop. At any moment, their pursuers might tire of waiting at the maze entrance, and extend their search round the foot of the hill. If they came, there was nowhere here to hide.

But no riders appeared, and they plodded on until at last they reached a shadowy line of trees and plunged thankfully among the dark trunks.

'Go as fast as you can!' Cluaran cried. Edmund saw Elspeth grab at the rough mane as her mare broke into a gallop. With a surge of relief he spurred his own horse beside her, keeping one eye on Elspeth to make sure she didn't fall off.

Cluaran seemed to find paths through the trees that Edmund could not see. They never stopped and hardly stumbled, though he could feel his horse was tiring. He, too, felt light-headed with weariness. His arm and chin still throbbed, but the pain was dimmed by knowing they had escaped Glastening with their lives.

At last Cluaran led them out of the trees, into a misty drizzle under a lightening sky. He signalled to Edmund and Elspeth to dismount, and they led the steaming horses up a steep, wooded incline to a rocky overhang. At the back was a small cave where most of the rain did not reach.

Elspeth was stumbling with tiredness, and her face was taut and pale beneath her cropped hair. They tethered the horses and half-walked, half-fell into the cave, where they sat slumped together, their backs against the rough stone.

'You rode well,' Edmund murmured, his eyes closing.

'Least I didn't fall off,' Elspeth mumbled. Then all he heard was her even breathing before he too fell asleep.

Edmund dreamed he was back home in Noviomagus. He was five years old. His father was away. But Aelfred was at court with Edmund and Branwen. It was the autumn before he had left for Gaul to buy six black horses. Edmund's uncle was a grown man by now, perhaps twenty, but that did not stop him running wild with Edmund by the lake. They had just been playing Edmund's favourite game – duelling with wooden swords till they scared the flock of stately white geese into fits of honking outrage.

In the next instant they were gathering blackberries. Edmund was running down an avenue of tall yellowing elms to the next bramble patch, his uncle pounding behind him. His hands and face were already sticky with purple juice, and the bowl he carried shook as he ran, spilling some of the fruit.

'Slow down, little Whitewing!' called Aelfred. It was his pet name for Edmund, taken from the white geese on the lake. Aelfred was brown-haired and dark-eyed like his sister, Branwen, and had always teased Edmund about his light colouring. 'Walk out in the snow and we'll lose you!' he would say. Now, as he caught up, he tutted at the purple stains around Edmund's mouth. 'We'll have to wash you before we go in – we'll never hide those from your mother!'

The bramble bushes were all around Edmund now. He held on to the bowl as his uncle lifted him up to reach the fat berries at the top. Spikes caught at his clothes and stabbed his arms. Ignoring them, he reached out for a shiny black berry – and recoiled. Looking down at him from among the grey-green leaves of an overhanging hawthorn branch was an eye; a bird's eye, gleaming round and black. The bird raised its head. It was a giant raven, rising above the bushes as it spread its wings. It cried once, harshly. Then, without warning, it came at him, beak outstretched.

His uncle's supporting arms vanished. Edmund tumbled backwards, arms thrown over his face against the stabbing beak and raking talons. He hit the ground hard and backed frantically away – but the attack did not come. Blinking, he saw the great bird flapping slowly away from him. It was dark. And the ground beneath him was not grass but stone.

He was in a large room, dimly lit and filled with strange objects he did not recognise: great machines of wood and iron. Their shapes were unfamiliar, but something about them filled Edmund with dread.

Suddenly one of them moved. He started back in panic, then realised that there was someone there. It was Elspeth, standing pressed up against an iron bar. No – not standing. She was chained to it; her feet did not touch the ground. And she was struggling, crying out soundlessly, her face contorted in pain.

A hooded figure was approaching her from the shadows. It held out something in its hand – the glint of candlelight on a sharpened blade? Edmund lunged towards them both, his mouth open to scream – and found that he could not move. It was as if he was caught in brambles again. Something held him fast on all sides, although he couldn't see what it was. He fought to free himself, but he could not help her. Sick with helplessness he watched as the shadow drew closer.

CHAPTER FOURTEEN

Elspeth started awake. It was Edmund who had woken her – he had cried out. She looked at him, but he was still sleeping. Elspeth groaned as she stretched. Every bone ached and the muscles in her legs screamed when she bent her knees. The cave floor was damp and there was a steady drizzle driving under the rocky roof just a few feet away. Outside the day was dull and grey, making it impossible to tell how late in the day they had slept.

She watched Edmund, wondering whether to wake him. His hands plucked the air and now and then he moaned. He seemed thinner than when Elspeth had first met him on the *Spearwa*, and older too, as if the last few days had worn him down. His face glowed white through the walnut stain, and the cut on his chin looked sore and swollen.

Then the memories of their last night's escape came flooding back. Elspeth sat up, looking around for Cluaran. He was not there. She had seen how he had looked at the sword. He had known what it was, and for a heartbeat she

147

had seen his face blaze with excitement. But he had not mentioned the sword on the long ride to the cave, not asked her whence it came, nor how she had known it would slice through the pillars of stone and cut off the Guardians from their pursuit.

Edmund stirred, and she saw he was awake, staring at her. He looked upset, his blue eyes filled with distress.

'Elspeth!' he murmured.

'I'm here,' she said.

She saw Edmund shake his head as if to clear it. But before she could ask him about his dream, Cluaran came into the cave, his cloak beaded with moisture and his hair plastered to his head.

'Spring weather,' he grunted, nodding towards the rain that was falling steadily behind him. 'But rain or not, we must leave at once. The Guardians do not give up the chase so easily.' He went over to inspect the wound on Edmund's arm. 'You'll have a scar,' he told him, 'but it's healing cleanly. Can you ride?'

Edmund nodded. Elspeth's heart sank but she followed the others to where the horses stood cropping the rain-swept hillside. Below them was a wide stretch of forest: tall oaks, beech and chestnut, their first leaves breaking, and beyond them, in the far distance, the brown gleam of a river.

'We're heading that way,' the minstrel said, pointing. 'Once over the river, it's two days' ride to Venta if we keep to the forest tracks.'

Elspeth climbed stiffly on to the old mare. Every footfall sent a twinge through her muscles but at least she no longer felt in constant danger of falling off. Gritting her teeth, she followed the other two riders through the trees. After a while Edmund fell back to ride alongside her. He held his left arm as if it still pained him, but even so, he rode with an ease that Elspeth could only envy.

'Grip the horse's sides with your knees,' he told her.

'I'd rather walk,' she confessed. 'I'll never want to sit down again after another day of this!'

'It feels like that at first,' he said. 'But you'll soon grow used to it, and that old mare is a steady beast. She'll not let you fall.' His expression changed, as if he had remembered something that worried him. 'The path is narrow here,' he said abruptly. 'I'll ride behind.' As he fell back she caught an odd look on his face: concern? But why should he worry about her? He was the one who was hurt.

They went down little-used tracks, the horses picking their way through last year's thickets and stretching their heads up now and then to snatch a mouthful of new shoots from the branches. Elspeth was just beginning to feel easier in the saddle when Cluaran's gelding pulled up suddenly, ears twitching and nostrils flaring. Her mare stopped too, whinnying in alarm. Cluaran dismounted and calmed his horse.

'Has something scared them?' Elspeth asked.

'Some wild beast – perhaps a boar. There are many of them in the forest.' Cluaran whispered into his horse's ear until it quieted; then leaped on its back and set off as briskly as before. The mare, though, kept her ears back and continued to turn head nervously.

Elspeth patted the rough brown neck and made what she hoped were soothing sounds. On a sudden thought, she called softly to Edmund.

'*Are* there wild animals near? Can you use their eyes?'

He cast a wary look over at Cluaran, who was riding some way in front. Then his face took on the inward look that Elspeth recognised from the night on the moor and the showman's booth in Glastening.

'Yes,' he said at last. 'There are wild creatures of some sort. But they're not watching us.'

Elspeth looked at him with fascination; what must it be like to see through the eyes of an animal? She would have liked to ask him more, but stopped herself with a glance at the distant figure of the minstrel.

'I hope we reach the river soon,' was all she said.

It was afternoon when they heard the sound of water through the trees.

'We'll ford the river here,' Cluaran called to them.

As they approached, the rain fell more heavily and a wind whipped up, spattering them with drops from the branches. Cluaran frowned when he saw the brown and swirling water.

'We must try to cross,' he said. 'The nearest bridge is several leagues away at Oferstow. After the way you drew attention to yourselves at Glastening, I think we should avoid the haunts of men.' He jumped down into the mud and signalled to Edmund to do the same. 'I'll try the depth first.'

Edmund took the reins of both horses while Cluaran waded into the murky flow. He was waist-deep in moments, but moved steadily onwards. Suddenly he staggered and vanished beneath the surface. Elspeth gasped – but he reappeared a moment later, now in water to his chest. He turned and called to them, but his voice was lost in the rush of the water. His eyes stretched wide and he pointed urgently behind them, into the woods.

Edmund spun round. Out of the trees came a low brown shape, then another; then four or five together. Blunt snouts. Small eyes lost in ruddy bristles. Pairs of curling tusks that gleamed in the dull light.

The wild boars advanced towards them on stubby, purposeful legs. Edmund saw Elspeth raise her right hand, the gauntlet flashing silver on her fingers, but in the next instant the mare had bolted, carrying Elspeth off into the trees. The two geldings reared up, tearing their reins from Edmund's grasp. They took off after their stablemate, just as the boars closed in on Edmund.

Edmund had seen wild boar aplenty, and hunted them too, but he had never seen a beast as huge as the one that led this herd. It stood almost as tall as he was, its tusks flared out like scimitar blades. Edmund knew what they could do; on a hunt with a Sussex thane, he had seen a huntsman gored in the groin. The man had bled to death before he made it back to the thane's longhouse.

Edmund looked wildly around for a stick, anything to fend them off.

'*Don't try fighting them!*' Cluaran's cry reached him faintly across the water. 'Run! Climb a tree!'

The king boar charged. Edmund darted for the trees and leaped for a straggly alder, hauling himself up by the thin branches just as the boar struck the trunk.

The whole tree shook. Edmund scrabbled for a firmer footing on the wet branches, yelling out as he wrenched his wounded arm. Below him, the boars surrounded the tree, a dozen of them with their eyes gleaming like coals, tusks glinting like some devilish warrior force.

Edmund heard a blood-curdling yell; saw Cluaran running through the trees at full cry. Faster than light, he hurled an armful of stones at the boars. The smaller beasts fled, but the king boar stayed until one of the stones struck it on his forehead, between its eyes. It staggered back, its trotters gouging long scars in the muddy ground, before wheeling around and running into the forest after its herd. With a strangled sigh, Edmund slid down the tree and landed at Cluaran's feet.

Cluaran hauled him up, ignoring his yelp of pain as he grabbed Edmund's wounded arm. 'I've never seen the like of it,' he muttered. 'A boar that large defies all reason, unless –' He stopped. 'Still, we have more troubles than combating some giant swine. The Guardians will be on our trail by now. And here we are without our horses, my pack and the girl lost.' He frowned. 'Fool of a girl! She has the sword and yet she lets her own horse run off with her as if she were no more than a saddlebag.'

Edmund flared. Doubtless he was grateful to Cluaran for scaring off the boar, but for this rag-tag minstrel to insult the girl who had saved them from the Guardians back at the Tor! It was outrageous. Why did he treat them like fools?

'I can find her!' he cried. 'Right now!'

Cluaran stood stock-still, his look caught between mockery and something else, something thoughtful and questioning.

Edmund glared at him. He'd show this scornful man just what he could do, who he really was. He leaned against the tree and closed his eyes, casting his mind out to find Elspeth, or her horse, or some woodland creature that was watching them now.

Suddenly he was with them – twelve beasts galloping fast. The world was leached of colour, but wider than he had ever seen it; the forest stretching out on both sides as if blinkers had been taken from his sight. He could see the rippling flanks of his herdmates: the tree trunks streaming away, the grasses crushed beneath their feet. His gaze was focused on the legs of a bolting horse. Then on a figure standing on a path. Elspeth! Why was she off her horse? Had she fallen? There was something else too – a tiny blur at Elspeth's feet –

Edmund pulled himself back with a jolt and opened his eyes. With horror he knew he'd been looking through the king boar's eyes.

'Quick!' he cried to Cluaran. 'This way!'

It was no good. Elspeth couldn't hold on much longer.

When the mare had bolted from the river bank, she had carried Elspeth back into the forest, swerving round trees, plunging through bushes. Low-slung branches had whipped Elspeth's face and she had flung herself against the horse's neck, clinging to the mane for dear life.

On and on. The forest turned to a green blur. Elspeth felt she had been riding for ever. *I've lost the others*, she thought.

At last the mare began to slow but, just when Elspeth thought she was regaining control, the horse dug in her hoofs and stopped dead. With a cry, Elspeth shot forward, grabbing up the reins as she slid over the horse's neck. She missed the thorn patch and landed in a clump of bracken. The mare danced away, and almost at once, Elspeth flew to her feet, clinging to the reins. *What was wrong with this horse?*

'It's all right, girl. Hush, slow down now.'

The mare quietened and Elspeth brushed herself down. Something caught her eye on the forest path, barely the length of a man away from her. A flash of red-brown, too bright to be a fox. She took another step and gasped with surprise.

It was a child! Perhaps four or five summers old, too young to be all on her own in the forest. Was there someone with her? Elspeth looked around, listening hard. No one came. She watched the red-haired child crouched at the side of the path, carefully gathering fragments of broken eggshell into the lap of her skirt. She was humming to herself, and a wing of hair had fallen forward over her cheek, hiding her face.

'Hello there!' Elspeth called.

The child started and dropped a piece of eggshell. Before Elspeth could say anything else, the mare shied and yanked the reins out of her hands.

Whirling around, Elspeth stared in dismay as the king boar plunged out of the trees and charged along the path with its head down and strings of saliva streaming from its tusks.

Without a second thought, she stepped into the boar's path, and shot out her arm: *Come!*

With a hiss of sliced air, the crystal sword burst from her hand. Behind her, she heard the child gasp with surprise as the grove flooded with light.

'Stay back!' Elspeth screamed over her shoulder. Only a few more paces and the boar would be upon them.

Its herdmates had veered into the trees, squealing, when the light of the sword dazzled their eyes, but the king boar hardly broke its stride.

'God help me!' Elspeth cried, lunging forward.

The trees beside her rustled and she braced herself for another charging boar, knowing she could never fight off two of them.

Instead, Cluaran and Elspeth leaped on to the path between her and the king boar. Cluaran loosed arrows, one, two, three, so close together Elspeth could not see his hand reach back to the quiver between each one. Edmund held a log in his hands, flailing it so that it knocked into tree trunks and sent twigs and leaves showering down around him.

The king boar faltered as Cluaran's arrows struck home, lodging in its massive shoulders, and swerved sideways to dodge Edmund's club. On it came, towards Elspeth and the child.

Help me! she prayed.

And a voice like fire and ice together answered, *I am here. Do not be afraid.*

Steadying her right hand with her left, Elspeth brought the sword down towards the boar, feeling the air slice beneath the shining blade. She closed her eyes and braced herself for the jarring impact of blade on flesh and bone – but felt nothing. She opened her eyes again. At the last instant, the king boar had veered away and bolted into the trees, leaving only a trail of quivering leaves to show where it had once been.

'Are you all right?' Edmund demanded, running over to Elspeth.

She nodded, too breathless to speak. She had called the sword, and it had answered her. And this time she had been closed it again with a tiny shake of her head. Edmund let out a long breath; with the luck of the gods, she would think she had been dazzled by a flash of sunshine. Everything had happened so fast, it was hard even for him to recall the moment of attack.

The horses were found, and Cluaran came into Kedwyn's hut, bringing with him the smell of the forest: earth and damp leaves and a lingering scent of boar. He was followed by Bergred the blacksmith, who clicked his tongue at the state of the horses.

'They're done in,' he said, 'and that mare's all but lamed! You'd not have gone much further on these three.' He insisted that they took their supper at his home, which was larger than Kedwyn's. 'There's not a family here that hasn't had someone killed or hurt by those evil boar. And now you two lads have driven the brutes off! There's many will want to shake your hands for that.'

So much for not drawing attention to ourselves, Edmund thought.

They drank barley-mutton broth from wooden bowls, sitting around Bergred's hearth with his two sons. Later, other villagers drifted in. The talk turned again to the boars' attacks on the villagers, and Edmund listened in growing horror as Bergred recounted the tales.

'They stalk us like devils,' he said. 'We dare not enter the forest for firewood with less than six of us. They seem to know. Lie in wait. That king boar, he leads them.' He counted out the death list on the fingers of his powerful hands: a simpleton boy found dead and partly eaten in the middle of winter; a

prepared to use it. She would have killed the boar to save the child. She swung round and saw Cluaran scoop the girl into his arms. The child was speechless with shock, her blue eyes wide and scared.

'She must have come from Oferstow,' he said. His voice sounded oddly expressionless, and his gaze darted to Elspeth's right hand, where the sword was flickering like a snuffed candle.

Then Cluaran sighed and said quietly, 'Like it or not, it seems we are bound for Oferstow after all.'

CHAPTER FIFTEEN

Edmund held out his hands to the blacksmith's fire and smiled. He caught Elspeth's eye.

'Cluaran has a strange idea of misfortune!' he whispered.

She grinned back. It was wonderful to be warm and dry again, to have good food and the promise of a dry bed for the night.

Cluaran had made it clear that they must move on at first light. He was perched on a wheel hub on the far side of the forge hearth — set to spring for the door any moment. But Edmund decided he was just being Cluaran, unhappy at the press of too many friendly people. For all that he earned his living entertaining the guests of great halls across the land, it was clear the minstrel was happy with no company but his own, and trusted nothing but what his own eyes saw.

Fifteen or so villagers had arrived on the forest path soon after the king boar had fled. They came beating the trees, grim-faced and calling, searching for the lost child. A broad-beamed woman with fox-coloured hair had snatched the child from Cluaran's arms as if she suspected him of child-stealing, but Elspeth and Edmund were quick to tell them about the wild boars — leaving out only how Edmund had tracked the herd through the forest, and how Elspeth had managed to scare the king boar away. To their relief, the little girl said nothing about the blade of light that had sprung from Elspeth's hand. In fact, she said nothing at all, merely burying her face in her mother's arm and hunching her shoulders against the horrors that dwelled in the forest.

The boy's mother, the red-haired Mistress Kedwyn, had bade the lads, Elis and Edmund, to come straight away to her village house, while the menfolk, armed with bows, went with Cluaran to find the lost horses. There was blood trickling down Elspeth's face from a cut where a branch had hit her, and with Edmund's wounds, it won them a heroes' welcome.

'The leader of that herd killed my husband two years agone,' Kedwyn told them, her eyes clouding with pain at the memory. She set the girl on a folded blanket by her hearth while she fetched a pot of salve. Then she dressed Elspeth's cut brow, and cleaned and tended Edmund's wounds. Edmund flinched when she smeared the salve on to his broken skin.

'It burned like fury,' he told Elspeth afterwards. 'But my arm feels better already.'

The girl stared at the flames, and then at Elspeth's hand. Edmund glanced at Elspeth; she looked uneasy at what the child might say. The girl opened her mouth as if to speak, then

farmer who lost his hand when a pack of the brutes attacked his three-year-old son, and later died of gangrene; Bergred's own eldest son, gored two winters before; a babe snatched from its basket set in the field's shade at harvest time . . .

The sad catalogue ran on as Mistress Kedwyn came in with a jug of ale. 'They took two souls that day. Maesgarad's baby first, and when Bergred and Toby gave chase, Toby too was taken. Swift as the wind, young Toby was . . .'

'And I as slow as winter,' Bergred said heavily. 'He was dead when I got there. Gored through the belly. But I saw that great black beast standing high as my waist, and I tell you I saw malice in his eye, like I'd been looking into the eyes of a black-hearted man. Vengeance, that's what he wants. Vengeance and death.'

'But why?' Edmund whispered. 'Why do these boar behave like this?'

For a time no one spoke – and that made it plain they knew the answer. At last, as if by silent agreement, Bergred began.

'There is no reason not to tell you. You've had your share of them.'

They came as a punishment, the blacksmith told them. There were some who said they were supernatural beasts conjured by sorcery. There were others who claimed the Guardians had simply rounded them up and driven them here to Oferstow forest.

At the mention of the Guardians everyone in the room had looked anxiously at the door. But it stayed closed – and the fact that Cluaran alone had not flinched made Edmund more easy.

'Are you saying the Guardians brought the boars?' Elspeth questioned, puzzled.

Bergred nodded. Two years ago, he'd been called out in a filthy storm to help an old man whose mule cart had stuck in the mud by the bridge. The axle had split, and Bergred had taken the man and his goods into the byre while he mended it. The old man had been in a stew of worry, begging Bergred to help him hide the cart's load under the hay. Bergred had thought the man cracked; why would anyone want to hide firewood and sacks of oatmeal in an honest village? But that wasn't it. Concealed within the load was the strangest-looking chest, bound with hasps of iron, and a lock with no place for a key. The old man made the blacksmith swear to secrecy; to tell no one of its presence while he was in the village.

Elspeth felt her hand tingle, and she clenched her fingers tight into her palm. She had seen that chest for herself – had opened the sealed lock and reached inside to pick up a silver gauntlet that even now burned beneath her skin.

'The old man offered me a dozen silver coins to work through the night,' Bergred went on. 'It's for the good of Wessex, he told me.'

Elspeth risked a glance at Edmund and read the same understanding in his eyes; the old man was Thrimgar, and he had stopped at Oferstow on his desperate flight from Venta Bulgarum.

'The next day at noon, but a quarter-day since I'd seen the old man leave, the Guardians came galloping in, led by Orgrim himself. 'Tis not often we have a man from the King's Rede among us, yet I freely say I did not take to him.' He broke off as Kedwyn shot a worried glance at Cluaran.

The minstrel inclined his head. 'Have no fear on our account,' he said. 'We do not trade secrets with the likes of him!'

The blacksmith struck his fist hard upon his wooden bench, and Elspeth nearly fell off her stool. 'And I believe you're honest!' he cried. 'But someone had spied on us on that day. Orgrim knew Thrimgar had been sighted here, knew I was lying when I said I'd seen no such old man. Who told him, no one knows. It could only be the birds!'

Edmund tensed. Bergred did not really blame the birds, that was obvious. What man would think birds could spy on humans? But birds had eyes, and a Ripente could use any creature's sight as easy as drawing breath . . .

'So Orgrim sent the boars as a punishment?' said Elspeth.

'We cannot doubt it,' Bergred replied. 'Orgrim was in a fury that day. I could see from his face that he knew I was lying, but with the old man long gone and no sign of his load in my byre, there was nothing he could do. As he rode out of Oferstow, he told us we would have good cause to regret helping a traitor. That forest looks like fine boar-hunting territory, he said.'

'And then the boars came,' Elspeth whispered, and Edmund saw a silver sheen thrumming on her hand, which she kept tightly clenched in her lap.

Brooding afresh on their misfortune, the villagers began to leave. Elspeth heard the blacksmith tell Cluaran the horses needed at least another day's rest before they'd be fit to ride again. She saw the minstrel frown, but Elspeth felt her heart leap.

'Don't you see?' she whispered to Edmund. 'This is our chance to help these people! We can find the boars, and trap them. And,' she added, her eyes burning, 'we can pay back Orgrim for Medwel, like for like.' When she saw the answering gleam in Edmund's blue eyes, his grim smile, she knew he agreed with her.

Cluaran was asking the blacksmith if he had any horses they could borrow in place of their lame nags, but Edmund broke in.

'We'll be glad to stay another day, Master Bergred.' With a glance at Elspeth, he went on, 'Master Cluaran is a skilled tracker. If we could find the boars in the forest, and surround them with archers –'

' – we could dig a pit and drive them into it,' Elspeth finished. She looked up at Bergred, her face alight. 'We could kill all of them at once!'

Bergred and Kedwyn looked at each other. 'No,' Kedwyn said. 'It's a fine idea, but we couldn't let two young boys like you risk yourselves.'

But Bergred clearly thought differently. 'We'll not risk the lads, of course,' he told Kedwyn, 'but it could work.' He turned to the minstrel. 'What do you say, Master Cluaran? Are you as good at following creatures through these woods as your boy says? For I tell you: do this for us and we'll give you the best horses we have in the village.'

Cluaran narrowed his eyes at Edmund. 'If my apprentices are set on trying where so many have failed, I'll not stop them. But I'd want one of the boys with me to help with the tracking,' he said, and Bergred nodded. 'I make no promises,' Cluaran warned, 'but if I have your word on the horses, I'll do what I can.'

Cluaran and Edmund made their way cautiously into the trees at first light. Behind them, six village men walked in a line, armed with bows and knives.

'We may as well go hunting with a herd of cattle for the noise they're making,' Cluaran grumbled, signalling to the nearest man to tread more quietly.

They had left Elspeth with Mistress Kedwyn. Edmund had wondered why Cluaran was so insistent she stayed behind; after all, he knew about the sword. Surely that would be a matchless weapon against the boars? But something in the minstrel's expression warned them he would brook no argument – either Elspeth stayed behind, or they wouldn't go at all.

'So,' Cluaran said quietly, when they had drawn a little way ahead of the line of men, 'you mean to be a hero in spite of all sense. You're Ripente, aren't you? That's how you found Elspeth yesterday.'

Edmund nodded defiantly.

But Cluaran only looked thoughtful. 'It's a skill that can

make you enemies; you are wise to keep it hidden. How well-practised are you with it?'

'Well enough,' Edmund replied stiffly, not ready to admit he could count the times he had used his unlooked-for gift on both hands.

They walked through the forest until they reached the deadfall that the villagers had spent all night digging, ready to trap the beasts. Edmund eyed the sharpened stakes fixed along its length, each one tipped with a gleaming spearhead. The line of men joined them at the edge of the pit, fear chasing across their eyes like clouds.

Cluaran looked at Edmund. 'Now all we need are the boars,' he said drily.

He started to move away but stopped when they heard footsteps running through the trees. A moment later Elspeth panted up, carrying a skin of water.

'Mistress Kedwyn thought you might be thirsty,' she explained, handing the skin to the men.

'You don't lose me so easily,' she whispered to Edmund. 'I'll be close by, I promise!' He opened his mouth to protest, feeling sure Cluaran wanted her to stay behind for a reason, but she spun away to take the empty skin and trotted into the trees as if she intended to return to the village straight away.

Edmund went to stand beside Cluaran. The minstrel looked down at him with his eyebrows raised.

'She's gone back to Mistress Kedwyn,' Edmund muttered, feeling sure the lie was writ large on his face.

Cluaran didn't say anything, just headed into the trees. They drew ahead of the archers again.

'The boars are not far off. I can smell them,' Cluaran whispered. 'Can you find them?'

Edmund closed his eyes and tried to concentrate. Cluaran was right; he could feel them close by, but he could see nothing. He reached out further, more intently. He *must* find them! But there was nothing for his eyes to fix on to; only darkness.

And then, in the dark, a movement.

It was so faint he did not dare shift his gaze. The boars must be deep in the undergrowth, where no light yet reached. But there it was: the stir of a branch on one side of him – and on the other, so close he almost jumped, the gleam of an eye and the pale shimmer of a tusk. The boars were moving.

'They're in a dark place,' he whispered.

'Underground?' asked Cluaran.

Edmund shook his head. 'No, but there's little light. A thicket of brambles – they're walking close together, between branches.' He paused, blinking the creature's eyes to see more clearly. 'The land slopes down quite steeply, and there are stones underfoot.'

Cluaran hissed between his teeth. 'There is a ridge near here, further into the forest and well-hidden in undergrowth. That could be where they are.'

Edmund gritted his teeth. 'Lead me closer. I'll tell you if I see anything more.'

Keeping his eyes tight-shut for fear of losing the sight, he reached out to grasp Cluaran's arm.

It was a strange, halting journey. Cluaran steered him through the trunks and fended back the branches that whipped at his face. But the minstrel could not see the twisting roots that tripped him, nor the bracken that tangled around his legs. Sometimes Edmund heard the men following at a distance, but mostly he fixed on the dim movement of the boars and told Cluaran everything he could see – the slope of the land, a sudden brightness where the boars broke out of the brambles into a copse of birch trees, their trunks rising palely out of a sea of umber bracken.

'Yes,' Cluaran murmured, or 'I know where that might be,' and he gripped Edmund by the shoulders and turned him to walk in a different direction. Edmund stumbled on, letting his mind fill with nothing but the sight of the boar. There were deep-gleaming eyes on both sides of him now, and ahead the shadowy bulk of the king boar, leading them on.

Suddenly the huge beast halted, its ears twitching.

They can hear us!

Edmund halted. 'They're here!' he gasped.

The minstrel released Edmund so abruptly that he staggered. 'I can smell them,' he breathed in Edmund's ear. 'We're downwind of them – we'll not get a better chance to take them unawares.'

Edmund opened his eyes to a blaze of orange light. Blinking, he made out the figure of Cluaran silhouetted against the sunrise, raising his arm to signal to the men. There was a flurry in the trees behind them as the archers moved into position; then the minstrel gave the signal to move forward. Freed from the boar's eyes, Edmund felt as if he were looking down a tunnel: dizzyingly bright straight ahead; blind on each side. Shaking his head to clear it, he began to push forward, this time towards the great red disc of the sun, which winked at him as he moved through the trees.

There were yells ahead of him. He pushed through the underbrush to see the boars with his own eyes, dark shapes among the tree roots. The first arrows were already flying. One beast fell, squealing, and the rest turned to flee in panic.

Edmund fitted an arrow to his own bow and joined in the chase, driving the creatures into the rising sun. *I did it!* he thought joyfully. *I used my gift to find the boars!*

Through the forest they ploughed, tasting the fear of the boars as they were hunted like prey.

Suddenly, there was the clearing ahead of them. The pit in the centre gaped black in the red light, the villagers, spears raised, standing on each side of it like statues. There was a moment's awful stillness as the boars burst from the trees; then a great roar rose as men and women lowered their spears and rushed on the creatures, herding them towards the pit.

Edmund froze. There was one boar missing. Somehow the king boar had broken away from its herdmates, and left them to be preyed upon alone. *Where was he?*

Elspeth was waiting at the edge of the crowd, standing well back in the shadow of the trees. Her face lit up at the sight of Edmund. She raised her hand in greeting and started towards him as the villagers closed in on the pit.

And then a thin, high sound sliced the forest air: a single squeal, sharp as a razor. The king boar stood at the edge of the clearing, outside the ring of archers, black as pitch, its head lifted as if it revelled in the scent of blood and fear that hung among the trees.

For an instant only it stood, then it charged straight at Edmund.

He heard Elspeth screaming as if she were a long way away. He dropped to one knee, fumbling to arm his bow. The great beast seemed to come towards him with dreamlike slowness, its breath steaming in the damp air, its eyes gleaming like cracks in a furnace.

Steady, steady. Edmund pulled back the string and loosed his arrow.

It hit the boar in the shoulder, gouging a wound the length of a man's hand in the bristly flesh. The beast swerved and charged past Edmund, knocking him flying, heading instead for the archer closest to him. The man had no arrow ready. With a yell, he dropped his bow and dashed for the trees.

For an instant Elspeth's running figure flashed white against the tree trunks, held frozen as if in a shard of ice. Then she was pelting after the boar, the crystal sword blazing in her hand.

'Cluaran!' Edmund yelled, but Elspeth was already vanishing from sight among the trees. Edmund followed her for a few steps, then stopped, casting after her with his mind's eye.

Once more he was in a world drained of colour, the forest opening up on each side. He saw the village man's fleeing legs as he scrambled up a tree; felt the rush of rage; winced as the trunk rushed to hit him in the face. He had found not Elspeth, but the king boar. Now Edmund tried to make his body run too, while his mind travelled on with the boar's eyes. He had to reach Elspeth before she caught up with the boar.

Then white light sliced through the trees behind him, and he knew he had found her.

He felt the boar's fear as it whirled around to face the shining white light. This was not an enemy it understood, but it would fight to the death. Behind the light stood a small, furious human figure. The sword rose into the air and the boar rushed forwards to meet it.

Now! Edmund thought. *Now! Let her strike a blow at Orgrim!*

He jerked forward as the death-blow struck his neck. He fell on his face, gasping. Rough hands seized him and yanked him upright. Ahead of him he could see the giant boar slumped to the ground with a gaping wound in its neck. Elspeth was bent over the beast, panting as the sword faded in her hand.

Someone spun Edmund round.

Cluaran.

'Do you not know the limits of your gift, you fool?'

CHAPTER SIXTEEN

'What kind of a Ripente are you?' Cluaran cried.

Elspeth had never seen him so furious. When there was no reply, Cluaran grabbed Edmund and shook him. Edmund stared dumbly back.

'You borrowed the eyes of a creature about to die!' Cluaran hissed. Behind them, the rescued archer was climbing shakily down from his tree. Elspeth thrust her right hand behind her back before he saw the blade of light, feeling the weight of the sword slowly leaving her.

Cluaran lowered his voice and gripped Edmund hard by the shoulders. 'The boar's death would have blinded you, boy – taken your sight for ever! Has no one taught you these things?'

Edmund's face was bloodless under the walnut dye. Cluaran glared at him a moment longer and released his shoulders with an explosive sigh.

'No, I see you're as ignorant as you look. It's a wonder you've survived this long.' He turned abruptly to Elspeth and the Oferstow man. 'If you can walk, we should fetch the others,' he called. 'They'll want to see this for themselves.'

The archer looked down at the dead boar and then at Elspeth, wide-eyed. 'A true monster,' he said. 'And you killed him, lad.'

''Twas a lucky blow, sir,' Elspeth mumbled, ducking her head and running after Cluaran and Edmund. She wanted time to think. Her heart was pounding like a drum. Triumph. Awe. Terror. They beat a tattoo against her ribs. She flexed her hand as the gauntlet's silver links dissolved once more into her flesh. She had used the sword to kill. She had summoned it and the sword had answered her. *This is what I was made for*, it seemed to say.

The archer caught up with her. 'Such a blow!' he marvelled. 'That's a good sword you have! 'Twas not forged in these parts, I'll warrant.' He broke off and frowned. 'Where is it? You've not left it with the carcass, have you?'

Elspeth stopped. She could not tell the truth about the sword, yet she felt unwilling to lie.

'It's not really mine,' she said evasively.

A sharp, throbbing pulse shot through her arm. *I am yours for ever, Elspeth*, said the voice.

Word that one of the minstrel's boys had killed the king boar spread like fire, and when the great beast was brought into the village slung from poles, cheers went up for all three of the visitors. Elspeth caught Cluaran's eye and knew they had drawn more attention to them than was safe, even without any sign of the Guardians. As the villagers gathered to roast two of the boar carcasses over a bonfire, she went looking for Edmund and found him sitting on the ground by the smithy, staring morosely into the distance.

'We should be celebrating,' she murmured, sitting down to him.

'How does Cluaran know so much about my power?' Edmund burst out, as if he hadn't heard her. 'I almost lost my sight for ever when you killed the boar. I was starting to think I could control it – even use it to help people. And now it seems I don't understand it at all.'

Elspeth took his arm. 'You *have* helped Oferstow,' she said. 'Look at all this!' She gestured towards the bonfire, the people dancing in the light of the flames, and he brightened a little. 'Cluaran has travelled everywhere and knows everything, it seems,' Elspeth said lightly. 'But it's *you* who is Ripente, not he.' She clambered to her feet, holding out a hand to him. 'We'll have to leave soon,' she told him. 'We should say goodbye.'

Bergred and Kedwyn tried to persuade them to stay for the feast, but Cluaran politely refused. 'We still have a way to go,' he said, 'and we're in some haste.' He hesitated a moment. 'If the Guardians come here asking about us, you'd be wise not to say you gave us hospitality.'

'They won't hear of you at all,' Bergred promised. 'Not from us.'

Bergred exchanged three sturdy young geldings for their spavined horses and they left before the sun had started to dip towards the horizon. The villagers gave them other gifts: hooded cloaks lined with wool, and enough food and drink to last them as far as Venta Bulgarum.

They stayed away from the road for the first day and into the second, camping for the night in a glade of trees beside a stream where they could wash and water the horses. Cluaran seemed to know the route well, and Elspeth wondered how many times he travelled these ways. The invisible paths they followed didn't pass near any settlements where he could earn food and shelter, so it seemed an unlikely route for one who lived as a minstrel.

Late on the second day, he led them out of the trees on to a rocky hillside. From there they looked out on well-tended fields, and beyond these Elspeth could see the brown curve of the road.

'There's a crossroads just past that turn,' the minstrel told them. 'The road runs straight east to Venta, half a league's distance and patrolled all the way.' He pointed to a patch of paler green among the trees below. 'The horses can rest there,' he said, 'and you'll stay to watch them. I'm going on foot from here.'

'You expect us to stay here?' Elspeth demanded.

'You're going openly on the road?' asked Edmund.

Cluaran did not answer either of them. Instead, he turned his mount and trotted a short distance along the hillside. As

Elspeth and Edmund followed, more of the road came into view below them. Elspeth saw where it crossed another, smaller track. The minstrel gestured down towards the cross-roads, to a tall wooden structure with something dangling from it.

It was a gibbet. Elspeth swallowed hard as she saw what looked like a bundle of rags swinging gently from the rope. There were executions at home in Dubris, of course, but her father had not been a man to take his child to a hanging. Elspeth crossed herself and murmured a prayer for the hanged man's soul. Beside her, Edmund was very still.

'That's why I'm taking the road,' Cluaran said over his shoulder. 'The Guardians make sure there are plenty of hangings here as warnings to folk tempted to stray from the patrolled paths. Any traveller who does not keep to the road is likely to be taken and hanged as a thief – particularly if he's armed.'

'Is there something terrible in the woods, away from the paths?' Elspeth asked, feeling a tremor of fear.

Cluaran looked at her strangely. 'No. But it suits the Guardians to keep the townspeople afraid. And the corpses of strangers make useful threats.'

They rode downhill in silence. The little patch of green that they had seen from above was little more than a clearing in the forest, an untended stretch of tall grass and scraggly weeds.

'This is the last common ground before Venta,' Cluaran

told them. 'Stay near the trees, and if you hear riders, leave the horses and hide.' He dismounted with a leap. 'If anyone else comes by, tell them you're minding your master's beasts to save him stable charges.' He smiled thinly. 'The townsfolk will believe that.'

'Why do you have to go to Venta, anyway?' Elspeth challenged. The minstrel walked on as if he had not heard her. 'And why can't we come with you?' she shouted after him. 'We can take care of ourselves!'

Cluaran turned to look at her. 'You'd bring the Guardians down on our heads within a quarter-day,' he snapped. 'There is something I must find in Venta, and I'll not have you distracting me with your near escapes. You know full well that you have what Orgrim wants more than anything else.' He nodded at Elspeth's hand, but she was so stunned by his direct reference to the sword that she did not reply. 'Wait here until I come for you,' he said, and he vanished among the trees.

Elspeth started after him. The wood here was only a few yards deep. She came out of the trees to see the minstrel striding over scrubby grassland to the road. He did not seem to be hurrying, but Elspeth could not catch up with him. She stared after him crossly.

A hand grasped her shoulder and pulled her back into the shelter of the trees. 'What are you doing?' Edmund demanded. 'Didn't you hear what he said?'

'I don't care,' Elspeth said. 'He's no right to leave us behind like . . . like baggage! What is this thing that he has to find?

Why can't he tell us? Doesn't he trust us?' She kicked angrily at a stone, sending it spinning across the brittle turf. 'Not that I trust him either, for that matter! Always sloping off at night, acting like we're no better able to take care of ourselves than babes. It's not fair!'

'Let him be,' Edmund said. 'You're right, Elspeth. He treats us like servants, or naughty children. We can take our horses and go east without him, around the town. But don't follow him. It could be dangerous.' His voice grew harder, more urgent, and Elspeth looked at him in astonishment. He seemed to hesitate, then went on in a rush. 'I had a dream two nights ago. I didn't know where I was – but someone had hold of you, someone evil, and he was hurting you. I'm afraid that if we go into Venta, it will come true.' He went on, not meeting her gaze: 'I know it sounds foolish. But I said nothing when I had a vision of the soldiers attacking Medwel, and it turned out to be much more than a dream. I couldn't forgive myself if something happened to you.'

'I don't think you're foolish,' Elspeth said carefully. She didn't doubt Edmund – or, at least, she didn't doubt that he genuinely believed she was in danger – but she still burned with curiosity to know what Cluaran was doing, and that more than any fear for her own safety made her desperate to go into town. 'But how do you know the bad thing won't happen if we stay here?' she went on persuasively.

'I suppose you could be right,' he said at last. 'We'll go in together – as long as we're careful.'

'I'll creep like a mouse,' she promised, and ran back through the trees to check the horses were tethered.

When they first emerged from the trees they felt horribly exposed. But as they started to follow the road towards the town, they felt more at ease. At the crossroads Elspeth quickened her pace. The gibbet with its grisly load creaked above them and she could not resist a glance upwards, wondering what the poor man had done to draw down the wrath of the Guardians . . . or was it a woman? It was no longer possible to tell.

'What will we tell the guards, if we meet any?' Edmund asked her quietly.

'What Cluaran told us,' she replied. 'We're servants, left behind by our master. Too poor for anyone to bother with.'

The walls of Venta Bulgarum were made of huge wooden stakes, sharpened to points. The massive gate was closed and barred with iron, and the men standing with spears by the wooden guardhouse were as unwelcoming as the gate they guarded.

'Halt!' one of them snapped as Elspeth and Edmund approached. 'What's your business?'

'Our master left us to take care of his horses,' Elspeth explained, putting a whine into her voice. 'But he gave us no food, and we're hungry!'

The man gave a bark of laughter. 'He should have known

better than to trust a pair of idle young louts!' he snorted. 'And you think you'll get a meal by following him, not a whipping? Your master's horses are worth more to him than you are, I'll wager!'

He opened a small wicket in the fortified gate and let them through. 'If you want to get yourselves beaten, I'll not stop you,' he said as they hastened inside. 'But you'd better find him before curfew.'

The houses came right up to the walls of the town, the road branching between them. The outermost buildings were small and poor, with wattle-and-daub walls, crammed together and linked by a spider's web of paths. Elspeth and Edmund took the road that seemed widest and straightest, and soon came among larger houses, with vegetable patches and fire pits outside. Elspeth could hear chickens clucking from outhouses, and she saw an old woman milking a goat, but there were few people about. Cooking smells filled the air, and she could hear voices from several of the window slits. She guessed most of the town were at supper. Beside her Edmund was looking around warily, but now that she was here Elspeth felt an overflowing confidence, as if nothing could hurt her. It was the way she had felt when she had used the crystal sword at Glastening, and at Oferstow, when it had flashed into brilliance almost before she had called it, had seemed to *answer* her . . .

'Well, we're here,' Edmund said. 'We'll find Cluaran and see what he's doing – though I'd rather he didn't see us.'

'He'd only look at us down that long nose of his,' Elspeth agreed.

'And tell us again how important his business is, and how we hinder him,' Edmund added. He laughed briefly, then his face was sombre again. 'Even so, we don't want to be recognised,' he said.

His seriousness sobered Elspeth at once. 'I'm not planning to do anything stupid,' she tried to reassure him. 'If there's any chance of meeting the Guardians, we'll hide.'

As if to challenge her words, there was a clatter of hoofs behind them.

Edmund grabbed her hand and drew her into a cluster of houses. They slipped around the corner of the nearest building – a rich-looking home, with stout wooden walls and good-smelling cooking steam rising from the smoke hole. They crept along its walls away from the road as the sound of the riders drew nearer, then rattled away. The sun was low in the sky, and in the shadow of the houses it was almost dark. They skirted vegetable patches and middens, meeting no one except a couple of girls drawing water at a well. The girls glanced at them curiously as they passed.

A bell tolled from somewhere ahead of them and the girls hastily wound up their bucket and hurried inside.

'That must be the curfew bell,' Edmund said. He stood still for a moment. 'I've been trying to look through Cluaran's eyes, but I can't find him. Where do you think he's likely to be?'

Elspeth looked up, over the roofs that surrounded them. Ahead, dark against the pale sky, were taller houses, and a tower that looked like stone.

'That way, I think,' she said. 'Whatever business he has here, it's likely to be in the centre of town.'

A narrow street led them to a broad square space lined with buildings much bigger than the outlying houses, and all of them built in stone. The tower that Elspeth had seen belonged to a church, larger and finer than the one they had seen in Glastening, but it was not the finest building in the square. The Romans had built here, and their work could be seen in the stone buildings on two sides of the square; they stood lower than the church, but were pillared and carved with a magnificence that dazzled Elspeth's eyes.

On the third side was a house of wooden beams, longer and wider than any home she had seen before; *like a king's hall*, she thought, as she crouched with Edmund behind a marble column. And only then did she see the men standing guard, their faces and dark clothes in shadow; the silver bosses on their shields reflecting the rays of the sinking sun.

The last few people abroad were moving purposefully out of the square: two women with baskets; an old man driving his goat; a little boy with a scrawny brown dog running at his heels. All of them were keeping to the edge of the square, giving the Guardians wide berth, and all were hurrying. Then Edmund caught Elspeth's arm and pointed. At the far end of the square, drawn back into a doorway, stood Cluaran.

The minstrel was gazing in the direction of the great hall. Elspeth wondered how long he had been there; he seemed as still as the stone itself. Then a movement in the corner of the square drew her eye. There was a clatter of hoofs and two Guardians rode up to the hall, carrying burning torches. Beside her, Edmund stiffened as if braced for flight – but the men only rode along the long building to place torches in the iron brackets at each end and on either side of the great door.

Then one of the riders saw the old man with the goat. He had almost reached the far end of the square, beating the reluctant animal with a switch to make it move faster. One of the horsemen called to the other, who chuckled. Then both spurred their horses up to the goatherd.

'You're out after curfew, old man!' one of them called. 'Will you pay the penalty now, or spend the night in the stocks?'

The old man stammered something that Elspeth could not hear. The second horseman laughed. 'No money?' he crowed. 'What need of that, when you have this fine beast?' Still laughing, he leaned down to grab the rope around the goat's neck.

The two Guardians outside the hall had strolled over to watch. The old man started whimpering, his arms around the goat's neck as he pleaded with his tormentors. Glancing at the marble doorway, Elspeth saw that Cluaran was no longer there.

He was running towards the hall, swiftly but keeping to the cover of the stone columns. None of the Guardians had noticed anything; they were gathered around the old goatherd, the two on foot grabbing his arms. He let go of the goat, which gave a bleat of terror and bolted, nearly dragging its captor from his horse. Cursing, the rider dropped the rope and called his companion to join the chase.

The goat's mad rush took it into Cluaran's path. Seeing someone there, it bleated loudly and veered away. The Guardian holding the old man released him and he ran after his goat. Then the four Guardians, no longer laughing, advanced on Cluaran.

'What's this?' asked one of the horsemen, while the other spurred his horse to the end of the colonnade to cut off any retreat.

Cluaran stood where he was and waited for the Guardians to encircle him. He held his harp in one hand, as if he was about to play a tune. Something in his profile looked faintly amused as he lounged against a stone pillar.

'Is something wrong?' he asked.

The rider barked an order to the men on foot, who ran up to seize Cluaran's arms. 'You're a stranger here,' the horseman said harshly. 'Skulking in the streets after curfew – and armed. You're a danger to the king.'

'You mean my bow and skinning knife?' Cluaran said in mild surprise. 'I'm a minstrel, masters! I travel far to carry out my trade and must eat on the way. Look.' Elspeth did not see how he managed it, but in one fleet movement Cluaran stepped away from the two pairs of hands holding him, and raised the harp. 'I'm sorely grieved to have given alarm to the town's brave defenders,' he said. 'Let me give you a song.'

He swept his hand over the strings. As the first notes echoed around the square, the two foot soldiers let their hands fall and stepped away from the minstrel, shuffling back dream-like until they were standing beside the pillars.

The horseman lunged forward and dashed the harp out of Cluaran's hands. It struck the stones with a discordant jangle, shockingly loud in the quiet square.

'Hold him, you witless oafs!' he roared. The two men blinked and jerked forward to seize the minstrel again. 'I've heard enough from him,' the Guardian snarled. 'He's a vagrant and a troublemaker.'

'Should we take him to Captain Cathbar, sir?' asked one of the foot soldiers.

'That old fool!' sneered the horseman. He bent down from the saddle and lowered his voice. 'Listen, oaf. You don't have anything to do with Cathbar, right? Don't give him your prisoners; don't ask his help. Lord Orgrim doesn't like the man, understand?'

The foot soldier nodded frantically.

'So,' the Guardian went on thoughtfully, 'we can't take him to Cathbar – and there's no point bringing a beggar like this before his lordship. We'll just string him up right now.' He reached behind him and produced a coil of rope from his saddlebag.

Time seemed to stop. Without any sensible thought,

Elspeth found the crystal sword blazing in her hand. It sent a shock of pain up her arm, jolting her forward. Edmund cried out and tried to hold her back, but she was already running across the square.

I didn't summon it, she thought as she ran. *Did I?*

The faces of Cluaran and the Guardians were white blurs in front of her. She lunged first at one Guardian; then the other. Both sprang back, fumbling for their own swords. She thought one of them was wounded, but a moment later both men came at her. She swung at the nearest attacker, clumsily – then the crystal blade seemed to twist in her hand, blocking the second sword as it snaked in from the side. But the first man had already recovered – he was coming at her again. The crystal sword was whipping towards him, but her hand was slow behind it and her body too heavy to dodge.

There was a sharp *thwack* and the first man fell back, a feathered shaft protruding from his shoulder. The second attacker was backing away too, his eyes wide as he looked past Elspeth to the other end of the square, where she had left Edmund. Edmund with his bow and quiver of arrows, which he had brought into the town beneath his tunic.

Behind the two foot soldiers, Cluaran had caught up his harp and was running back down the colonnade towards the arch of the door. He leaped, caught hold of the great stone lintel and pulled himself lightly up. The next time she looked, he was taking aim with his own bow. She gripped the sword more tightly, hearing its voice shriek within her: *I am yours, Elspeth! I will fight for you!*

But her surge of confidence was short-lived. Next she heard Edmund's voice, shrill with panic.

'Elspeth! The horseman – behind you . . .'

Then something cracked into the side of her head and she found herself spreadeagled on the stone paving, her arms held on each side. She could hear Edmund's cries as he fought behind her, but they were fading. Through the red mist that filled her eyes she saw Cluaran leap upwards again, on to the roof of the massive stone building; he threw a last agonised glance at Elspeth – no, not at her but at the *sword* – then disappeared.

And just before the world went dark she saw, against the twilit sky, a great black bird hovering above her. Its single harsh cry sounded like laughter.

CHAPTER SEVENTEEN

They had been tied together back-to-back, so Edmund had no way of knowing how badly Elspeth had been hurt. He knew she was alive because he could hear her breathing. She was slumped against him, her chains digging into his back. The sword had vanished like a blown-out candle after the horseman knocked her down. Nevertheless, the Guardians had seen it clearly. They had muttered together, looking over their shoulders at the hall, and sent a servant for chains and manacles before they would approach her. Edmund, his arrows spent and with no other weapon but his fists, had only merited ropes.

He had fought them anyway, determined not to be taken anywhere without Elspeth. But as he struggled, he had felt a small, searching pressure in his head, faint but horribly familiar. He shut his eyes to push it aside, close up the smoky gap in his mind – and by the time it was gone, his captors had him securely tied. It was only then that he heard the harsh cry and looked up to see Lord Orgrim's great black bird hovering over them.

Now, sitting in the dark on the packed-earth floor of the prison hut, Edmund wondered wretchedly what was the use of having a crystal sword and the gift of Ripente if they could still be trussed up like pheasants.

A commotion sounded outside: loud voices and heavy, hurrying feet. Edmund tensed, willing Elspeth to wake up as the footsteps approached. Then he realised that the voices were quarrelling.

'This is Guardians' business, not yours. You've no call to come here.'

'And I say I have.' The second voice was deep and rather hoarse; it sounded familiar to Edmund and he tried to recall where he had heard it before. 'My men have been hunting the villains as well as yours, and I was a king's man when you and your Guardians were herding your mother's geese! If these two have threatened the king, it's my right to see them.'

There was a scraping noise as a cover was drawn back from a spyhole in the door. When the deep voice spoke again it was indignant. 'It's just a pair of boys!'

'I can't help that, Captain Cathbar,' said the other man, sounding defensive. 'Lord Orgrim says they're murderers. One of them had a sword. I can't let you go in there!'

'Try to stop me, lad. You'll rue your actions, I can promise you that.'

The heavy door was flung open and Cathbar shouldered his way in, holding a torch in one hand while with the other he slammed the door shut behind him. Outside, Edmund heard the Guardian hurrying away.

'He'll be back in a while with a few more of them,' Cathbar said. Edmund recognised him at once; it was the man who had been searching for them by the lake on the day they crossed into Wessex. In the light of the torch his face was lined and tough-looking, with deep-set eyes staring coolly at Edmund.

'And then they'll throw me out,' the captain continued, 'but not before I've had a word with you. You're not what I expected, see.'

'I'll talk to you,' Edmund said carefully. From the conversation he had just overheard, this man was not one of the Guardians, though that didn't mean he could trust him. 'I'll ask your help first. My companion's hurt.'

'I'm all right,' Elspeth said faintly behind him. Relief swept over Edmund as she stirred. The chains clanked and she hissed through her teeth with pain. 'My head!'

Cathbar crossed to her in one stride, studying her face in the torchlight. 'You neither of you have the look of desperate assassins,' he said. 'They say you came into the town with weapons and attacked the Guardians.' He looked Edmund square in the face. 'Will you tell me if they're right, and why you came here?'

'No,' Edmund said steadily. 'Not until you tell us what the Guardians mean to do with us.'

The man sighed. 'As to that, lad, I can't tell any more than you. I'm one of the king's men, not a Guardian. But I have heard that Lord Orgrim has called a trial tomorrow in the Rede House – that's the great stone building in the square, where the king and council meet. It's my guess that the trial's to be yours, and the charge will be conspiracy against the king.'

There was a silence. Edmund felt his spine turn to ice. Against his back Elspeth was suddenly rigid.

'I'll not lie to you,' Cathbar went on. 'Innocent or guilty, there's little enough I can do for you. But if you came to Venta for some good reason, tell me, and I'll see that the court hears of it.'

'We're not here for any reason,' Edmund said dully. 'We were walking east to go home, that's all.'

'And I insisted we came into the town for nothing more than curiosity,' Elspeth put in bitterly. 'I should have listened to Aagard. He *said* we should beware of Venta.'

Cathbar was very still. 'What name did you say?'

'Aagard,' Edmund repeated cautiously. 'He's an old man who helped us when our ship was wrecked.'

'Tell me, what was he like?' The captain's voice held an edge of excitement. Half to himself, he muttered, 'There cannot be two of that name, surely?'

'Tall, with a white beard and very dark eyes,' said Edmund. 'He's a scholar and a healer. He said he had once been in the King's Rede, and he had a red robe –'

'I saw him in it, many times,' Cathbar interrupted, 'though his beard was barely streaked with grey when I knew him.' He looked sharply at Edmund. 'Where did you leave him? Is he well?'

Edmund gave the captain a brief account of the start of their journey, not mentioning the dragon or his vision.

'Aagard heard that a village we had passed through was attacked by soldiers,' he said. 'He went back to help them, and we travelled on.'

Cathbar was silent for a while. 'I believe you,' he said at length. He lowered his voice. 'Did Aagard tell you why he left Wessex?' He must have seen the answer in Edmund's face. 'It was a black day when Orgrim accused six of the King's Rede of treachery. I knew Aagard would never plot against his lord.' His voice so soft now that Edmund could hardly hear him. 'I was one of the men sent to arrest Aagard and Thrimgar. I let them escape and told the king they'd already fled.'

'What happened to the others of the Rede?' Edmund asked. 'Did they escape too?'

Cathbar grimaced. 'Hanged, every last one of them.' He stared into the distance for a moment, then straightened up and turned back to Edmund and Elspeth. 'Orgrim's hanged too many good men. And now to bring a couple of boys to trial . . . No. The king has to see reason this time.'

Looking at the man's grim face, Edmund came to a decision. 'You know I'm unarmed,' he said. 'Would you free my hands? There's something I'd like to show you.'

Cathbar looked into his eyes, then drew his knife and cut the rope around Edmund's wrists. Edmund reached into the folds of his cloak for his name-clasp.

'We would never plot against your king,' he said. He held

the silver bird out to Cathbar. 'My father is King Heored of Sussex, and a friend of King Beotrich. If you would give this to the king, I think he'll hear our side of the story.'

For an instant Cathbar stared as if thunderstruck. But he recovered quickly, stepping back and shaking his head.

'Put your jewel away – yes, I know it, and if you've the sense your father has, you won't offer it again to a man you've only just met, even if he does wish you well.' He looked around him, then came close to Edmund and spoke quietly. 'I'll carry your message to the king. Perhaps even Orgrim would think twice before offending your father's kingdom. But make no mistake, it's he who has the king's ear now, and no one else. Don't be too hopeful.'

Footsteps and angry voices were approaching outside. Cathbar turned and left without another word, bolting the door behind him with a clang. Edmund thrust the silver clasp back inside his clothes, wound the rope around his wrists as well as he could and slumped against Elspeth.

'Captain Cathbar!'

Edmund shuddered. It was the voice of the horseman who had struck Elspeth to the ground last night.

'You disobeyed my direct orders.'

'That I did,' Cathbar agreed readily. 'After chasing these spies all over the kingdom, I felt it was my right to go in and talk to them.'

'I see.' The Guardian's voice was thoughtful. 'And what did they tell you?'

Edmund went cold. He had trusted Cathbar with the secret of his identity! Was the man going to betray them?

'They told me nothing about anything.' Cathbar's voice was scornful. 'It looks to me like you have the wrong pair. It's nothing but a couple of half-grown boys!'

Weak with relief, Edmund heard him walking away. Heavy footsteps came up to the cell door. Edmund stayed very still as someone uncovered the spyhole. They were presumably satisfied by what they saw, for no one else came into the cell, and after a time the footsteps moved away.

'How is your head?' Edmund whispered to Elspeth.

'Better, I think.'

Edmund busied himself with trying to loosen the rope around their waists, and after a while they were able to move a little. They dragged themselves to the edge of the cell and leant side by side against the wall. Watery moonlight filtered into the cell through chinks in the logs and under the door, but there was nothing to see, neither bedding nor chair.

Elspeth would not look at him and, stealing a glance at her, Edmund saw that her face was twisted with misery.

'This is all my fault,' she murmured. 'I *would* come here, even when you warned me not to. I'm sorry, Edmund!'

'I wanted to come too,' he told her. 'And my father really is a friend of King Beotrich. If that captain passes on the message, we'll be in no danger.'

He had spoken with more confidence than he felt, but it seemed to cheer Elspeth. 'The captain believed you, didn't he?' she said. 'And he said he was the one who freed Aagard. I think he'll keep his word.'

'Unlike Cluaran,' Edmund said bitterly. 'You saved him, and he deserted us!'

'Aagard did tell us not to trust him,' Elspeth reminded him.

'He didn't say he'd betray us!' Edmund could not keep the thought to himself any longer. 'Elspeth – suppose he knew we'd follow him? This could have been a trap!'

'No!' Elspeth's face was set. 'It was the sword that gave away who we were – it appeared without being called. Cluaran couldn't have known it would do that.' Her voice faltered. 'Could he?'

Elspeth was awake at first light when the Guardians came for them. She had hardly slept. Her arms were painfully cramped in the manacles, and her thoughts had given her no rest. Cluaran may have abandoned them, but wasn't it the sword that had betrayed them to the ones who had been searching for them all the way from Dunmonia?

The door burst open. Two dark-robed figures grabbed her chained arms and yanked Elspeth to her feet, untying her enough that she could walk. Behind her, Edmund was receiving the same treatment.

'Mind your clumsy hands!' came his voice, clear, loud and indignant, and Elspeth smiled. He *won't be cowed by a row of judges*, she thought.

They were taken outside and led to the pillared building on

the far side of the square. It was as high as a church inside, stone-built and echoing, with pillars along each of the two long walls. Edmund and Elspeth were marched between them, past empty benches to a platform at the far end on which sat seven men on great carved chairs. The Guardians pushed Edmund and Elspeth down to kneel on the floor.

For a moment the men on the platform looked at them in silence – and with some surprise, Elspeth thought. Then the man in the centre rose to his feet. He looked only a little older than Elspeth's father, with smooth yellow hair falling to his shoulders and a face that was pale, as if he rarely went into the sun. He wore a thin gold band across his forehead, and his robes were fastened with a brooch in the shape of a sword. At the sight of him, Edmund lifted his head and made to rise, but the Guardian behind him pushed him down so heavily that he sprawled forwards on his face.

This must be King Beotrich, thought Elspeth. *The most powerful man in the southern kingdoms.*

'Where is Orgrim?' the king demanded. He peered down at Elspeth and Edmund, then called down the hall again. 'Where is my chief counsellor? Are these the two spies I was told of?'

There was a stir at the back of the hall, followed by measured, heavy footsteps. As Elspeth twisted her head to try to see, she felt her right hand begin to burn beneath the skin. She shut her eyes and willed the sword to be still. With her hands bound, there was nothing she could do if it sprang to life – and she could not risk Orgrim knowing his prize was so close. If it came when she summoned it, surely she could tell it to stay hidden?

The newcomer walked slowly by them. Elspeth could see only a tall figure wearing the red robe of the king's counsellors. A fur-lined hood hid his face. He stood beside them, facing the council, and when he spoke, his cold, clear tones jolted Elspeth back to the lake in the forest, where they had hidden from the soldiers. This was the man who had been hunting for them across three kingdoms. This was Orgrim.

'My lords, these two prisoners were caught trying to enter the king's hall with a weapon. Their companion escaped and is being hunted by the Guardians. I have ordered a double guard around the king and council until he is caught.'

There was a buzz of agitated conversation on the platform. Beotrich frowned, his knuckles whitening as he gripped the carved wooden arms of his chair.

'Once again you show your care for my safety, Orgrim, and I am grateful. But what is this plot against us? We are at peace with all our neighbours, are we not?'

'Indeed we are, my lord,' Orgrim agreed. 'But I have discovered that the traitor Aagard is still alive and plotting against you. These two spies,' he gestured towards Elspeth and Edmund, 'were seen travelling with him.'

Raised voices sounded at the back of the hall.

'And I tell you I must be heard now!' It was Cathbar, roaring over the men who were trying to stop him. Elspeth saw the king flinch as the captain strode down the hall and stopped next to Edmund. 'Your pardon, my lord,' he said breathlessly, 'but this won't wait. These tales of spies and plots may be true for all I know, but these two have no part in them.' He laid a hand on Edmund's shoulder. 'This lad here is the son of your old friend Heored of Sussex. He's shown me the proof. I beg you at least to hear his story – you'd not condemn a king's son without hearing evidence on his side?'

Before the king could say anything, Edmund jumped up, his eyes blazing. They had bound his hands again, but he fumbled at his throat and brought out the silver bird, holding it up two-handed.

'It's the truth,' he said. 'I am Edmund of Sussex, and I pledge my father's friendship and my own to King Beotrich.'

Cathbar started forward as if to say something else, but Orgrim made a tiny gesture with his hand and two Guardians stepped forward, daggers drawn, to hold the captain where he was.

The king stood up and came to the edge of the platform to look more closely at Edmund.

'He does have a look of Heored,' he mused. 'Orgrim, perhaps there has been some mistake –'

'No!' Cruel fury flashed through his words. 'Remember, my lord, I can see through people's eyes, know what they're thinking.' Beside Elspeth, Edmund's eyes narrowed as if he wanted to protest, but Orgrim went on relentlessly. 'A king's son can betray and spy as well as a churl – and with more reason! Who would be better placed to overrun your kingdom once you were dead, my lord?' Beotrich seemed about to protest, but Orgrim would not be stopped. 'Why else would they come – both of them – in disguise? This boy has darkened his hair and skin!' He pointed contemptuously at Elspeth. 'And *this*,' he said, '*this* is a girl, unnaturally concealed in men's clothing.'

Elspeth's right hand felt as if it was about to catch fire; she clenched it shut. *No*, she begged. *You must not come.*

I must!

Orgrim strode over and took hold of Elspeth. A great shudder ran through her and the sword burst from her chained hand in a blaze of brilliance.

Orgrim leaped back, a trickle of blood running from his wrist where the sword had caught it.

'Not just a traitor, but a witch as well,' he hissed.

'No!' Edmund shouted. 'Elspeth's no witch, and no spy either!'

Elspeth willed him to be quiet; it could do no good to speak for her now. But the men on the platform had no eyes for Edmund. Everyone was staring at the sword, burning white-hot in the dim chamber, held in a girl's resolute silver hand.

'By speaking for her, you convict yourself,' Orgrim told Edmund. He turned to Beotrich. 'Your verdict, my lord?'

The king looked horrified. 'Guilty, yes, of course,' he said, his eyes still on the crystal sword. 'I leave the sentencing to you, Orgrim.'

'You can't do this, my lord!' shouted Captain Cathbar.

Orgrim ignored him. 'Let the boy be taken back to his cell to await execution,' he ordered.

There was a shocked murmur from the bench. 'But, my lord,' quavered one of the old men, 'to kill a king's son –'

'He was sent here in disguise,' Orgrim reminded him. 'Hardly the mark of an honest visit, surely?' The counsellor was silent, and Orgrim went on. 'We need have no fear of what Sussex might do in response. King Heored is campaigning in the North and is not expected to return. His queen holds power in his absence. Could a woman lead an army to attack the might of Wessex?'

The Guardian behind Edmund hauled him to his feet. Other hands fell on Elspeth.

'Not the witch.' Orgrim stepped towards Elspeth, and she could feel the gloating in his voice as he looked down at her. 'There is more that she knows and has not revealed.' His lip curled. 'Take her to the stone cell and shackle her. I shall question her myself.' He swept a low, graceful bow to the king and council and strode from the hall.

Elspeth looked at the fading shard of light in her hand.

You should have helped me! she screamed silently. *Now Orgrim knows you are here. Is that what you wanted?*

CHAPTER EIGHTEEN

The tiny cell seemed even bleaker by daylight. Edmund had tried the door and scoured the timber walls for any weak points. Useless! It was built to keep in stronger prisoners than he, perhaps even those not bound hand and foot. There was nothing he could do but wait. They would not come for him till evening, he told himself; for if Venta's hangings were a public spectacle, they would not be scheduled to interfere with the day's work. But whatever Orgrim had planned for Elspeth, it would take place in private.

Edmund closed his eyes again, trying to concentrate as he cast about outside for any new information. The guard at the door had been joined by another man, but there was still little to see through their eyes; only stubbly grass and the back of King Beotrich's great hall.

It was so easy to look now. Ever since he had borrowed the boar's eyes, Edmund had felt that he had mastered the trick of it. He could move from gaze to gaze almost without thinking; he could even control his own movements while he looked through another's eyes. And yet here in the cell none of it helped at all.

He wondered for the hundredth time where they could have taken Elspeth. *The stone cell*, Orgrim had said. The words meant nothing to him. He concentrated on sending his sight out as far as he could, first in one direction, then another. Someone pounding beans at a wooden table; a woman feeding chickens; a man on horseback – a Guardian, judging by his sleek horse. A wandering dog sniffing at a meat bone. There was the stone Rede House, seen through the eyes of a woman hurrying through the square. He reached further, inside the building, and found a slave boy strewing rushes on the flagstones. But there were no steps or trapdoors in the stone floor; nothing that could be a cell, and no guards in the building to watch prisoners. And, though he strained his sight in every direction, no trace of the glowing whiteness he had seen on the one occasion that he tried to use Elspeth's eyes.

Could she be dead? He pushed that thought away. Orgrim had said she was to be questioned. *She will be wherever Orgrim is*, he thought.

Orgrim had tried to reach inside Edmund's mind again when he made his entrance in the Rede House. Edmund had felt his presence at once. Orgrim had not wanted to see through Edmund's eyes, nor even to feel the shape of his thoughts, but to let Edmund know of his power. And he did know it! It had swept through him like a storm-blast; like screams of the sinking *Spearwa*; like the gaping, merciless grin of Torment; like the blackness of the drowning sea.

Edmund buried his face in his hands. Another thought came to him – the barest impression, like a dream that fades on waking. There was something else about Orgrim that he had noticed, something that pricked at the edge of his mind like a thorn in a shoe. Was it the way he strode into the Rede House, the way he spoke?

Edmund pictured the tall figure, his cloak the colour of blood. The raised hood meant Edmund had not even seen what the man really looked like. And yet there *was* some hint of familiarity. Was it just that he was Ripente, like Edmund? Much as Edmund recoiled from being allied to this man in any way, perhaps their shared skill bound them deeper than kinship, deeper than loyalty to any mortal king. And yet Orgrim had lied when he had told Beotrich he had seen through Edmund's eyes and read his thoughts; he had tried and failed to steal his sight, and must know that Edmund was Ripente too.

A grating sound outside the cell door brought him to his senses. Come to hang him so soon? He fought to control the trembling in his arms and legs. They must not see him for a coward.

Something thumped against the cell wall. Then silence. Edmund held his breath and sent his mind out beyond the door. One pair of eyes. They were looking at a Guardian lying dead, an arrow through his heart. He felt the watcher's sudden terror as the blade of a knife flew through the air towards him.

Now the terror was Edmund's own. *A creature about to die . . . it would have blinded you!* He pulled back so fast, the cell spun round and he staggered. And in the spinning wall, the door flew open and there was Cluaran.

Before Edmund could speak, the minstrel dragged a dead guard into his cell, waving Edmund to help with the second. Next he was pushing the guard's bow and quiver into Edmund's hands before peering round the cell door.

'All clear,' he mouthed. 'Come on.'

Cluaran locked the cell door behind them, then set off like the wind. Edmund struggled after. They dodged past the high-gabled mansions of the rich where house slaves swept and carried water, then on through Venta's poorer quarters. It was afternoon and the streets were busy with traders – women with baskets of loaves and men pushing barrows laden with casks.

At last Cluaran dived into a barn, and Edmund fell gasping against a mouldy hay stook.

'How did you find me?' he choked. 'Orgrim has Guardians searching for you everywhere.'

Cluaran smiled. 'They're easy to fool. Right now they're hunting me through a henhouse on the other side of town. Feathers everywhere, no doubt.'

Edmund eyed him with surprise. The minstrel looked as if he enjoyed the thought of pursuit.

'We have to find Elspeth!' he blurted out. 'Orgrim took her.'

The minstrel's face darkened as Edmund told of the trial. 'Fool of a girl!' he muttered. 'Why didn't she use the sword?'

Edmund turned on him, fuming with anger. 'If she hadn't used it when the Guardians caught you in the square, she'd be free now.'

''Tis true,' Cluaran said quietly. 'Then it is for me to rescue them.'

Edmund frowned. *Them?* Was Cluaran talking of Elspeth *and* the sword?

Cluaran jumped to his feet and began pacing the length of the barn. 'Where in these Haunts of Adam has he taken them?' he muttered. 'I know the town well, but I've never heard of a stone cell.' Suddenly he was standing in front of Edmund, so suddenly that Edmund shrank back.

'I know you cannot look through Elspeth's eyes,' said the minstrel, 'the sword will not permit you – but you could look through Orgrim's eyes, couldn't you?' When Edmund opened his mouth to object, the minstrel went on, 'I know it is hard for Ripente to use each other's sight. But you are more powerful than most Ripente. Will you try?'

Again the storm raged through Edmund's mind. Again he was falling, tossed between Torment and the drowning sea. No! Not Orgrim's eyes. He'd rather ransack every head in Venta – anything with eyes to see, from man to horse to dog to cat to skittering lizard and skulking rat – anything but trespass in that evil mind . . .

Suddenly Cluaran grasped his arms like a vice, and the crush of his hands conjured another scene. It was the dream Edmund had had after their ride through the maze: the hooded figure, Elspeth chained to some monstrous machine, the knife coming down . . .

And then he thought of Medwel and another dream whose warning he had ignored.

'I'll do it,' he said.

Edmund sat on the ground, leaning against the hay, while Cluaran watched by the door. Slowly, slowly he pushed out his thoughts, trying to find Orgrim. *What if I can't hide from him?* he wondered. *Won't he know that I'm trying to use his eyes, just as I know when he's using mine?*

But the thought of Elspeth on that dreadful machine drove him on, weaving among the citizens of Venta as his mind reeled out on silken lines, further than he had ever sent it before.

He knew it at once when he found it, felt his body wince at the cold, metallic cast of Orgrim's thoughts. He plunged onwards, and looked through the Ripente's eyes.

He saw a room walled with stone, not lofty and pillared like the Rede House, but low, square and gloomy. Torches burned in brackets, their smoke blackening the walls, and in one corner, a three-legged brazier glowed. The door was small and close-fitting; no chink of light beneath it.

Along one wall were rough-hewn shelves: a row of books, a pile of knives, spikes, straps, and other tools Edmund could not name. Then a perch on which sat a great black bird, still as stone. Orgrim went to the shelf and chose a knife. Its long blade gleamed red in the torchlight. He turned . . .

Edmund knew exactly what he would see next. His instincts screamed to get away. *Calm! Be calm!* his mind commanded. *Don't give yourself away.* He let his eyes follow Orgrim's. There in the shadows were the great, ugly contraptions from his dream: a long wooden platform set with straps; then ropes strung from a roof beam, and there, in an angled iron frame as tall as a man, hung Elspeth, crushed like a deer in a trap.

Her neck was held by a collar. Tight metal cuffs clamped her wrists by her sides, and two more held her ankles. She seemed unconscious, but as Orgrim drew near, her eyes opened. The crystal sword burst into her gauntleted hand, flaring uselessly against the manacle. Her mouth opened in a soundless scream.

Orgrim spoke but Edmund could not hear the words. Elspeth glared into his face. *She's so brave*, Edmund thought despairingly, *but all the courage in the world won't save her now.*

Then a voice came to him from outside: 'Edmund. What do you see?' He had forgotten Cluaran. He was meant to be leading the minstrel to Orgrim – but how could he tell where he was? He struggled to find his voice, eyes still fixed on Elspeth's furious, agonised face.

'She's in a room . . . dark . . . lit by torches. Maybe underground? But no ladder, no steps . . .' He broke off. Orgrim had torn the sleeve from Elspeth's right arm and was pressing the point of his knife into her skin. Her eyes widened in pain.

'He's hurting her!' Edmund cried.

'Tell me what else you see.' Cluaran's voice sounded calm, detached.

'The floor seems uneven . . . the roof too. There's a prop holding it up.'

Elspeth screamed.

'Stone walls,' Edmund told Cluaran fiercely. 'No – wait . . .' The wall behind Elspeth was not quarried stone – it was rough, like a cave wall. And there, where the prop was lodged on the floor – wasn't that packed earth?

'It's not a room – it's a cave! Or a hut set into a hillside. The stone gives way to rock and earth.'

'The hermit's lodge!' the minstrel cried. 'Against the town wall, to the north-east.' There was a sound of rapid footsteps and he was gone.

Edmund knew he should follow, but his eyes were drawn back to Elspeth. Blood was trickling from a shallow cut in her arm; her eyes were shut and she was sweating. He could see Orgrim's hands streaked with blood, making complicated gestures around the crystal sword, which seemed to pulse in time with the twisting, folding fingers. Elspeth seemed barely conscious, her face as white as the crystal sword.

From behind Orgrim's eyes, Edmund knew exactly what the sorcerer meant to do. He was tearing the sword from her. And then Elspeth would die.

Edmund gave a soundless roar of outrage – and Orgrim's thoughts turned from his task. Edmund felt the familiar, horrible pressure in his own mind – then froze with shock.

Welcome, little one.

Edmund struggled to open his eyes, but could not. With horror, he realised he was trapped. His own body had gone, and there was nothing but the scene before him.

You should not have meddled, the cold voice said. *What did you think you could do?*

Leave her alone! Edmund tried to scream.

But the voice laughed at him. *You must go now. I'll come for you later, little Whitewing.*

There was a violent shove – and Edmund was lying face-down in the barn, his mouth full of hay.

The world was a red blur of pain. Elspeth's trapped limbs throbbed and the knife cuts on her arm burned like white-hot flames. The cuts were shallow and deliberate, as if Orgrim had drawn some strange design on her skin. With every cut, her sinews screamed with more than pain. She could not tell at whose insistence the sword was still there. Had Orgrim summoned it? Or had the sword decided to appear to fight its own battle?

At first, each new cut had brought a new demand: 'What is the sword's name?', 'How did you come by it?' And finally the same one, over and over: 'Give up the sword willingly, and I will not need to harm you.'

Before the pain took away her speech, she had spat at him, 'Find out for yourself, if you're so wise.' But the handsome face hovering over her had remained calm. Nothing she could

209

say would move him, so she had shut her mouth, determined not to cry out.

When he saw she would not answer, he stopped speaking and began to chant and sway, moving in and out of her vision. All she could hear was an endless incantation. The crystal sword throbbed in time with it, and with each throb Elspeth's strength flowed out in a river of pain. She wondered how much longer she could last. Fear had left her long ago, but there was still anger. Such a stupid way to be caught, such a waste.

The chanting stopped. Elspeth floated back into consciousness, risked opening her eyes. As she moved her head, the brace that gripped it sent agonising shock waves down her spine. Orgrim was still standing over her, but he seemed to have fallen into a trance – staring into space, talking to himself. Elspeth sent all her will into her sword hand. The effort shot such a searing pain through her arm and shoulder that she sobbed aloud. She could not even lift the blade. *Father!* she thought.

Suddenly a voice filled her mind. Its sound was like the bright white of the sword itself; its edge glacial; its power a torrent's spate. The voice was ancient and achingly familiar, as if Elspeth had heard it in her heart for a hundred years.

He won't get the sword that way!

The words crackled like ice sheets shattering on a winter pond.

He'll just destroy us both. There's only one way a hero can pass on the crystal sword.

How? Elspeth begged. *Please, help me!*

You must want to give me up, said the voice. *And you don't want to, do you, Elspeth?*

Orgrim grimaced, and his whole body twitched. His eyes fixed on Elspeth again.

'You'll never take it from me!' she cried. She saw his eyes harden.

'Kill me like this,' she persisted, 'and the sword goes too. I have to give it up freely. That means I can't be bound, or . . . or damaged. If you cripple me to get the sword, you will cripple it too.'

Orgrim narrowed his eyes. Then he nodded. 'Yes. I have other ways.'

He loosed the strap around her neck and freed her feet. Elspeth crumpled to the ground as her legs gave way beneath her. Barely conscious, she wondered vaguely how it was that the crystal sword drew no blood from her, even though it had sliced hard across her knees.

She lay like frozen stone, thinking once more of death. Again the voice rang through her head.

Get up, get up! You have to help me!

Elspeth's head spun. When Orgrim turned and crossed to his rack of instruments, she began, cautiously, to pull herself up.

'You will give it to me freely?' Orgrim asked, turning towards her. She could hear the triumph in his voice already.

'I didn't say that,' she told him. (*Get up!* screamed the voice.) Slowly she pulled her legs under and edged on to her knees. Against all odds her legs held her, though her arms throbbed weakly. *Sword*, she said silently, *you must help me now.*

I will, cried the sword. *Strike now!*

Elspeth raised the blade and lunged at Orgrim's head.

He was caught off guard and the sword sliced into his temple. But before she could strike again, he leaped towards the brazier in the corner of the room and plunged his hand into the burning coals.

Elspeth stared in horror as he lifted out a sword of his own, with a blade that glowed like rippling blue flames.

'This is foolishness, girl,' he told her. 'I'll kill you if I must.'

Elspeth felt the crystal sword pulse in her hand. *Help me!* she begged.

And now the sword did. It led and she followed, lunging and slashing. Orgrim staggered sideways.

We've got him!

But, no. It was only a feint. In the next pass, he brought the blue blade down in an overarm slash that she could not dodge. The blade sliced into her right shoulder.

The pain made her dizzy and she tried to sidestep, but Orgrim pursued her like a snake, slashing back and forth. Elspeth parried but a sickening wave of pain shot down her arm as the two blades crashed. She fell back, and back again, as each parry sent jolt after jolt through the wound. And even though the crystal sword still guided her hand, she could feel its energy draining away.

The sword's energy, or hers? It was impossible to tell.

With one last effort, she lunged forward, struck under Orgrim's guard and caught him in the leg. He grabbed her wounded shoulder with his free hand and sent her sprawling on her back. Stars of pain burst before her eyes. She could not move as he loomed over her.

The last thing she saw was the blue sword bearing down.

CHAPTER NINETEEN

Edmund's mind was reeling. *Whitewing*, the mocking voice had called him. *Little Whitewing*. Only one person had called him that: the man who had compared him to the geese on the lake, his uncle Aelfred. Tall, handsome Aelfred, who had picked blackberries with Edmund and promised to tell him secrets . . . who had gone off to Gaul because his ambition could not be satisfied in his sister's husband's kingdom . . . and who had begged Edmund's mother to send the boy to him when he was older. *Of all the world*, Edmund thought, *Aelfred was the one she trusted to keep me safe.*

How could Aelfed be Orgrim? How could a man change so utterly from what he once was?

Thoughts clanged in Edmund's head. *Perhaps my mother had been blinded by her love for her brother; perhaps my father had not been there often enough to see the truth – but I should have known. The clues were always there, if I'd had the wit to see them.*

He remembered his uncle's eyes, cool and quizzical, laughing at Edmund's attempts to impress him on their expeditions. Edmund had climbed the tallest trees and found the most daring, ingenious hiding places in their games of hide-and-seek among the elms. But Aelfred had always found him at once. *He has been using my eyes for years*, Edmund realised bitterly, *sharpening his Ripente skills on me*. The thought filled him with fury, and he found he was on his feet. He fumbled in the hay for the bow and quiver that Cluaran had given him and darted out of the hut.

The minstrel had long gone. Edmund looked back and forth, deciding which way to go. He must get back to the square. The north-east road was bound to strike out from there. He could get his bearings to the hermit's lodge at the town's north gate.

He ran desperately, careless now of anyone hunting him. This was all his fault! All this time, Elspeth had been travelling with the very person who could lead her enemy to her. Edmund's uncle would always be able to find him, because they were connected by something more than Ripente. Maybe he had always known Edmund would be on the *Spearwa* with the sea chest – though he couldn't have known that Edmund would be one of only two survivors. He must have rejoiced when his nephew washed ashore with the chest, knowing that now he would be able to follow it wherever it went.

Edmund began to falter and the town wall was not yet in sight. He had to do *something*! But who knew what Orgrim could do to her in the time it took Edmund to find the hermit's lodge? And even then, what would he do, armed only with his bow and arrows? His uncle would be protected by a hundred sinister enchantments, no doubt.

Then revelation struck – with all the brilliance of the crystal sword itself.

I don't need bows and arrows – not when I can fight him from inside his own mind!

Edmund slowed to a walk and sent his eyes ahead of him, searching out his quarry once more. It was not long before he sensed Orgrim's presence. Yes, there was the familiar edge of evil thought. But this time Edmund sensed something else too – a fuzziness that tasted of iron, as if the man had thrown up barriers and defences about his thoughts.

He can't keep me out, Edmund vowed. *Cluaran was right. I will not let Elspeth die, not if I have the slightest chance to save her! Wherever Orgrim tries to hide his thoughts, I will follow.*

The blade sliced down on her right hand. Elspeth gasped, but the blade rebounded, skittered off the silver gauntlet.

'It protects you,' Orgrim said with a trace of awe. He hauled the iron brazier out of the corner and pinned her legs beneath its feet. Hot coals scattered round her, sparks scorched her knees while Orgrim trod heavily on her sword arm. 'So let's try this . . .'

Suddenly he stopped dead. His face contorted and he spat out strange words.

A small hope flickered inside Elspeth. 'Edmund,' she

murmured. One last time she tried to lift her arm from the floor. She felt the sword's power surge in her arm.

Now, Elspeth! Strike once more and we have him!

But before the blade left the flagstone, Orgrim came back to his senses, grinding his foot harder on her arm. Elspeth bit her tongue to stop herself from screaming out loud. She could not move her hand now, she could not even feel the sword that she knew still burned in her fingers.

'How can he do that?' Orgrim cursed. 'A half-grown boy!' He gave a low whistle, and instantly a huge black bird, which Elspeth had thought was a stone carving, flapped down from the roof and landed on his shoulder.

'Find him,' the man said softly. He reached out a hand to push the heavy door ajar and watched the bird go.

'I think you'll be ready to offer me your sword now,' he told Elspeth.

Elspeth's heart turned to ice. What would the bird do to Edmund? Was she alone?

You are never alone, said the cool voice in her head, but it was faint, like the wind off snow.

Come back! Elspeth called desperately, but there was no reply.

'Your pale-haired friend is coming to rescue you,' said Orgrim. 'Did I tell you I knew him as a child?'

Elspeth stared at him in disbelief. 'How?' she croaked.

Orgrim's lip curled in a smile. 'Edmund is my nephew. He was always a loyal little fool. He won't leave you here to die alone. Which serves me well, because there's one last thing he can do for me before he goes to meet his gods.'

Elspeth cried out and Orgrim laughed. 'You won't deny me the sword, will you, when your friend is strapped to the frame?'

He shoved the brazier aside and pulled Elspeth up, twisting her hands behind her as he dragged her to the wall where chains were set in the stone. Suddenly he paused, his eyes unfocused.

'There,' he murmured. 'We have him.' His fingers tightened on Elspeth's shoulder, sinking like talons into prey . . .

Dim torchlight burned in a pall of smoke as Edmund slipped behind Orgrim's eyes. Elspeth was sprawled on the ground, the blue blade slashing down.

'*No!*' Edmund screamed.

At once Orgrim's mind responded, pushing Edmund away. He felt the cold grip on his own mind. And a great force as thought-tendrils burst forth like a many-headed serpent, striking, squeezing, twisting. Edmund clung on grimly. The torch-lit room whirled before his eyes.

A bolt of lightning punched through his brain. Orgrim hurled him away. The stone room was gone and Edmund pitched forward, landing on his knees just outside the North Gate.

Edmund scrambled to his feet. He had lost. Tears of rage sprang in his eyes. He swiped them away in time to see a black bird swooping above him. He had seen it before, on the shore by the lake. Watching, watching, taking his master's eyes to spy on every corner of the kingdom. Orgrim's raven. The sight of its spreading wings filled Edmund with a burning fury.

You'll not gloat over me, watching me fail.

In a second he had armed his bow and fired.

Elspeth braced herself.

And Orgrim screamed. He let go of her, clapped both his hands to his face and staggered backwards, shrieking.

'Dark! Dark! Where are my eyes?'

For a moment Elspeth staggered too. But only for a moment. The crystal sword sprang in her hand, pulling her after the blinded man, and she followed it gladly. Orgrim drew his own blade, but his eyes stared out unseeingly and his face was blank with horror. Elspeth lunged at him once, and he stepped heavily backwards and fell.

Elspeth raised the crystal sword over her head. She was shaking with pain and weariness, but the blade burned with a sudden brilliance, like a shaft of sun.

Orgrim gazed up at Elspeth, his eyes black and dull.

The door of the cell was flung open and Cluaran stopped dead in the opening.

'Strike, girl!' The minstrel's voice rang through the dim room. 'It's the sword's destiny, Elspeth!' he insisted. 'This is what it was made for.'

Elspeth listened for the cool voice in her mind, but it was silent. The decision to kill Orgrim or spare him was hers alone.

She shook her head. 'What about *my* destiny?' She turned from the man on the ground and lowered the sword. It faded as she walked away. But Elspeth thought she heard one tiny whisper, on the cusp of hearing.

Cluaran! I have returned!

The sound of the bird's dying shriek echoed in Edmund's head and he shuddered as he ran. The houses gave way to grazing land, just beyond the town walls. A steep slope of scree rose ahead, and picking his way over the loose rocks, a long way in front, was the brown-clad figure of Cluaran. Edmund tried to catch up with him, but the minstrel was moving too fast. In another moment he had vanished among the rocks.

Edmund cursed. He could see nothing but stones now. What if he couldn't find the entrance to the hermit's cave?

Suddenly he realised he was being followed. Over his pounding heart, he heard the pounding of footsteps. *Not now!* he railed. He couldn't be caught by the Guardians now!

He swung round ready to fight, as the large frame of Captain Cathbar lumbered up the hill.

'All right, lad!' the captain gasped, mopping his brow. 'I've not come to take you back to the cell.' He jerked his head in the direction that Cluaran had gone. 'Just tell me. That skinny fellow up ahead – is he your companion? The man who got away last night?'

He must have seen his answer in Edmund's face, for he nodded without waiting for a reply. 'He's a cunning one, and fast, too. They're looking for him to the south of town. But I thought he'd likely come for you and the girl.'

'He's done nothing wrong!' Edmund began.

Cathbar held up a hand. 'I don't believe he has,' he said. 'I told you, the Guardians have been picking scapegoats for a while now, and I'll not see another good man hanged if I can help it. But I want a word with him. They tell me he was picked up outside Orgrim's quarters in the Rede House.' Cathbar's face was grim. 'It's Orgrim your man is spying on, isn't it? And anything he knows about that snake, I want to know too.'

Edmund had his breath back now. 'Come on, then!' he said, and sprinted for the hill.

He had scrambled a good way up the pebbly slope before he saw the stone wall of the cell. It was cunningly built into an outcrop so as to be almost invisible. Cluaran stood stock-still in the doorway, looking into the cave.

Before Edmund could call out, Cluaran stepped aside and Elspeth stumbled out of the cell. The crystal sword hung from her hand, its blade trailing on the ground, its glow barely visible in the light of the setting sun. Her sleeve was torn and her arm was red with blood that trickled down the silvery hand that still gripped the hilt.

As Edmund started towards her she stopped, took one gasping breath and collapsed. By the time Cathbar came pounding up, Elspeth was blinking up at Edmund.

'What happened?' Edmund prompted. 'What did he do to you?'

'He clutched his eyes and screamed that he was blinded,' Elspeth whispered. 'He had sent a raven to find you.'

'I shot it,' Edmund told her bluntly, and he remembered the bird's cold eyes watching him through the leaves all those years ago. He remembered his uncle's laughing brown eyes as he so swiftly discovered Edmund's every clever hiding place. Edmund grimaced at all the little betrayals. 'If I had known that bird was nothing but a spy, I would have shot it sooner,' he muttered. He turned miserably back to Elspeth.

'Your arm!' he gasped. Elspeth's forearm was disfigured with cuts. Not random slashes, for the blood was drying to show a strange spiral that ended with two jagged lines. Edmund and Cathbar gazed at it in horror.

'It doesn't hurt much,' Elspeth said dully, though Edmund saw her turn her head away. 'Orgrim was doing some kind of sorcery, trying to charm the sword from me.'

'He has the same symbol cut into his own arm,' Cluaran called to them from the doorway to the cell. The usual mocking twist had left his face. Instead he looked defeated and troubled. He held one arm across his chest as if he were hiding something in his tunic.

He hesitated, looking intently at Edmund and Elspeth,

then at Elspeth's right hand. 'You've both helped me more than you can know, and you've earned the right to hear more. You'd better come inside.' He paused, then added, 'You too, Cathbar. You're caught in this coil as much as they are.'

The stone room seemed very dark as Edmund stepped out of the late-day sun. He peered around with a shock of familiarity. He had seen these shelves of books and instruments before, dimly lit in the red glow of the brazier, the rough-hewn floor stretching into shadow at the back, and, looming out of the shadows, the dull iron of the great triangular frame, its leather straps and cuffs dangling open.

He shuddered, and moved closer to Elspeth. And then he saw the huddled shape at their feet. It was Orgrim, his robes torn, his hands bound behind his back. He were moaning, twisting his head this way and that as if he were trying to find a way out of the blackness that filled his eyes.

'You've bound him!' Cathbar's voice behind them was shocked.

'With his own chains,' Cluaran agreed. 'Even blind and weaponless, he still has the power to do harm. I fear that what he's already achieved will never be undone.'

'What do you mean? What has he done?' Cathbar demanded. 'There's many of us suspected he was up to something black-hearted, but you'll never prove it. The king trusts Orgrim with his life.'

'As to what he's done, I can't yet be certain. But if it's proof of something black-hearted you want, captain, just look around you.'

Edmund watched the soldier's gaze travel around the cave: to the machine of wood and iron where Elspeth had been strapped; to the sorcerer's sword that lay on the floor, its blade dull grey now the heat of the fire had left it; to the scars on Elspeth's wrist, scored through swollen skin; lastly to the man bent double on the floor, his face hidden by a fold of his torn and blood-stained cloak.

Cathbar nodded. 'Oh yes, we have him now.'

The minstrel bent down to his pack and stowed a small object wrapped in sackcloth that he had been clutching to his chest. He stayed there for a moment, crouching with his head bowed over the package. Edmund saw with astonishment that the minstrel's face was white, and when he spoke it was very quietly, to someone who wasn't there.

'I have found it! But I was nearly too late to save her. I'm sorry.'

Cathbar coughed and Cluaran looked up with a start, as if he had forgotten the others were there. Refastening his pack, he straightened up and crossed to a jutting stone shelf where there was a row of books propped on their spines. Elspeth and Cathbar followed him – but Edmund could not move from the chained figure on the floor. His face was a pale disc in the half-light, stripped of intelligence and arrogance.

Tentatively, Edmund reached out to probe the sorcerer's

eyes. There was nothing but shadow behind them; as if there were no mind there at all, let alone eyes to see through.

'Aelfred,' he whispered. The man turned his face away, saying nothing. Edmund left the shell that had once been his uncle, his mother's treasured brother – the man he was meant to join in Gaul! – and went over to the others, his eyes stinging.

'This is the one that started it all,' Cluaran was saying, pointing to a massive book. It was bound in black leather, turned greenish with age and mildewed at the edges. 'This is the book of necromancy that Orgrim stole from the Rede.'

Elspeth nodded. 'Aagard told us about it. He said that the book contains spells to summon dragons.'

Cluaran narrowed his eyes. 'Dragons – and more.' He ran his finger lightly down the spine, then snatched his hand back as if it had been burned. He scooped up the edge of the cloak and tucked his fingers inside before drawing the book from the shelf.

As he lifted it, another book fell away, smaller than the first. It seemed newer than the spell book but cruder, little more than a sheaf of stiff pages bound together with thread.

Cluaran held them muffled in his cloak. 'I will show you more, but not in here.'

He pushed past them out of the door. Edmund glanced back at the prone figure of Orgrim. *His own uncle, the summoner of dragons.*

A low sound was coming from Orgrim, as if he were gasping

for breath. Edmund made himself go back. He knelt beside his uncle, searching for something to say. He leaned closer, then recoiled in horror.

Orgrim was laughing.

'This book contains spells of summoning and binding – and charms like these have power all of their own, even on the page. Don't come too close, Edmund.'

Edmund had come running out after them. He looked upset, but Elspeth found her gaze drawn back to the crumbling book. Cluaran had set it down on a flat stone a little way from the cave. A puff of dust rose as he opened it, and Elspeth looked at the pages in sick fascination. She could not read, but beneath the tiny, crabbed writing were complicated, spiralling designs that made her think of the marks Orgrim had cut on her arm. In the cloud of dust, the patterns seemed to move on the page. Elspeth shuddered and looked away.

Beside her, Cathbar scowled. 'I never held with books,' he muttered. 'I'll go see if the man himself will talk.' He stumped back to the stone cell.

Edmund was looking over Cluaran's shoulder now. 'To raise . . . Torment,' he read haltingly. His eyes stretched wide. 'The dragon Torment?'

'The dragon,' Cluaran agreed with a sharp look at Edmund. 'You know of him?'

'I saw him,' Edmund said, very low. 'When the ship was wrecked.'

Cluaran nodded as if Edmund had confirmed something he had already guessed. 'Torment knows . . .' he paused, and tried again, '. . . the sword. It was the sword that imprisoned him in the Snowlands, five-score winters ago. Orgrim must have believed that because he summoned the dragon, he could control it. He really believed he could control an ice-dragon!' The minstrel's face twisted and his voice was hard. 'It is safer to have no knowledge at all, than a little used unwisely.' He closed the book – Elspeth saw that he still touched the pages as little as he could – and turned to the untidily bound sheaf of papers beside it.

'These are Orgrim's own spells,' he said, 'the ones he worked with his own hands. On the last pages . . .' he stared at Elspeth and Edmund, his face bleak, 'he was trying to conjure a god.'

'But that's blasphemy!' Elspeth gasped.

'Which god?' Edmund exclaimed.

'Listen, both of you!' Cluaran snapped. 'I never thought to tell this to anyone, but you must hear it. It concerns you, Elspeth. And Edmund too, I think.' Elspeth eyed the minstrel nervously.

'I'm not talking of the God your monks worship,' the minstrel said softly, nodding to her, 'nor any of the gods of this land. Orgrim was trying to summon one of the old gods, from before Wessex and Sussex were kingdoms, even before men walked this land. One of the first rulers of earth, sea and air.' His voice took on a soft, lilting chant as if he were speaking the words of one of his songs. 'There was one of them who wished to rule not only the earth, but all things on it. He waged war against his fellow gods to take their power as well, and when he failed, he tried to destroy what they had created. So they bound him beneath a mountain in the far North, confining his spirit where it could do no harm. His name was Loki, the wily one. And there he stayed, chained with enchantment in a pit of fire.'

Cluaran's eyes darkened. 'Men came to live on earth and made new gods – the ones your mother sacrificed to for your safe journey, Edmund, and the one who dwells in your gods-houses, Elspeth. The elder gods faded and died but Loki lived on beneath his mountain, growing in strength and malice. And at last he found a way to reach out to the human minds around him.'

'Orgrim,' Edmund whispered.

'No. The first time was a hundred years ago,' Cluaran corrected him. 'It was a black-hearted sorcerer, just like Orgrim. Loki promised him more power than he had wit to ask, in return for freeing him.' He gazed over their heads, watching something they could not see. 'The sorcerer raised armies and used the book of necromancy – this book – to summon dragons to march with them.'

'But there's no such things as dragons!' Elspeth blurted out.

Cluaran looked at her, his eyes unreadable. 'Just because you have not seen something does not mean it doesn't exist. Since mortals have had the strength to contain them, they have been imprisoned far in the North, where men do not live. Only the darkest of spells can break them free from the ice. When Loki's sorcerer joined them with his army of men, a terrible war was fought, and nearly lost by the ones who knew Loki would bring only death and destruction. That was when the crystal sword was forged.'

'My sword!' exclaimed Elspeth. Instantly, she wished to take the words back.

'Yes, Elspeth. Your sword. It was created to defeat Loki himself. It will cut through anything, flesh, metal or rock. But by this very fact, the sword is also the only thing that could free Loki, cut loose the chains bound by magic. In forging the sword, we knew we were giving Loki the chance of freedom as well as defeat.' His face clouded with what looked like grief. 'The first sword-bearer managed to resist Loki and defeat the sorcerer who had been helping him – but at a terrible cost. We bound Loki once more and the sword was taken to Wessex, until it should be needed again. And now it has come to you.'

Elspeth felt her skin chill with horror. 'Are you saying that I have to do battle with a *god*?'

'If Loki is rising again,' Cluaran insisted, 'the crystal sword is our only hope. And the sword gave itself into your hand.'

Elspeth shook her head wordlessly.

The minstrel started to speak again, but Edmund interrupted him. 'Just now, you said "*we* bound him". Did you play a part in the last defeat of Loki? But you said it was a hundred years ago . . .'

Cluaran turned sharply to him, and Edmund fell silent.

'You have a decision to make,' the minstrel said, ignoring his question. 'Whether to help Elspeth in her quest – for quest it is – or go back to Noviomagus and hope that whatever evil forces Orgrim has released do not reach that far. You have a choice, while Elspeth does not.'

This is foolishness, Elspeth told herself, *all this talk of destiny and gods. I am no hero!* She felt the sick feeling swell in her stomach.

'Why should I have anything more to do?' she cried. 'Orgrim failed, didn't he? We kept the sword from him – so how could he raise Loki now?'

'A summoning this great has many stages.' Cluaran broke off, looking up the hill. Cathbar was trudging towards them. 'I'll tell you all I can,' he promised, 'but not now.'

'He won't talk,' Cathbar reported. 'Tis not just his sight he's lost. His mind's wandered also, though where it's gone I have no wish to follow.'

'Aelfred,' Edmund whispered.

Elspeth reached out and clasped his hand. There was nothing she could say to comfort him – she couldn't even imagine what it must feel to know your own kin had been responsible for such terrible things. Had she done the right thing, letting the sorcerer live? It might have been more merciful to Edmund if she had killed Orgrim, to spare him the shame of seeing his uncle blinded and maddened by the evil he had wrought about him.

Yes! It was my destiny! said the voice inside Elspeth, and her hand burned like ice and fire together.

CHAPTER TWENTY

The square before the Rede House was crammed with people, like bees buzzing in a hive. Many in the north-east quarter of the town complained of seeing a blinding blue light in the sky and hearing unearthly screams. They had come to demand what the king and his chief counsellor were doing about it. Edmund saw that the Guardians were patrolling the edges of the square, but they seemed ill at ease, with none of the blustering authority they had shown the day before. None of them made any approach to the excited groups of townsfolk, and no officer appeared to be giving orders.

Cathbar led the travellers straight to the king's hall, ignoring the little knots of people who tried to block their way. Edmund, walking behind with Elspeth, caught snatches of conversation.

' . . . heard crashing sounds from the king's hall, aye, and shouts too,' an old man was saying to his neighbour. 'They do say he's been murdered in his bed, and now . . .'

Cathbar quickened his pace and Edmund lost the rest of the sentence as he ran to keep up.

The Guardians standing outside the king's hall made no move to stop them as Cathbar hammered on the massive oak door.

'Barred from the inside,' he growled. 'We'll try the guards' gate.' He stepped back, but at that moment the sound of angry voices came from within the hall. A bolt grated on the other side and the door was flung open.

It was King Beotrich.

He lunged forward and gripped the captain by both shoulders. 'Cathbar! Some madness is happening. Where is Orgrim? Has he executed the boy who claimed to be the son of Heored of Sussex? I need to see more evidence that he is the spy Orgrim accuses him of being before we commit to such a harsh punishment.'

Cathbar stood like a rock, his eyes fixed on the king's face. 'My lord,' he said calmly, 'I can put all things to rights.' He reached out a hand to pull Edmund towards him. 'King Heored's son is safe – he is here. It is Orgrim who is the traitor, not this boy. I will bring Orgrim to you, and all proof you'll need of his dark intentions, if you'll give me the authority.'

King Beotrich looked uncertain. 'But Orgrim is my most trusted Redesman. He would not betray me, or my kingdom!'

'My lord, he would. Trust me, in the name of our God and

all that is holy.' Cathbar pointed at the Guardian officers. 'These men will not help me. They serve Orgrim, not you.'

The officers were keeping well back, but the commotion had drawn other listeners; a crowd of curious townsfolk was beginning to gather around them. Some of the Guardian foot soldiers who had been patrolling the edges of the square had hastened up as well. Many eyes were watching when King Beotrich turned to the ring of dark-clad officers.

'I herewith give full command of my household to Cathbar, with orders that he bring me the counsellor Orgrim.' He turned back to Cathbar, his eyes troubled. 'You have been in my service a long time, Cathbar,' he said quietly. 'Please God you are not lying to me.'

Cathbar held his gaze without flinching. 'You may take my life if I am.'

The king nodded.

For a moment there was only stillness, then a babble of excited voices that rose to a roar. The little ring of officers looked at each other in consternation. The Guardians at the back of the crowd began to move away.

Cathbar turned to Cluaran, pulling a seal-ring off his finger. 'Go to the guardhouse behind the king's hall; find a man-at-arms called Alberd and show him this. Tell him that he's to gather my men and bring them here at once. Armed.'

Edmund exchanged a look with Elspeth. Cluaran would not welcome being ordered around like a serving boy! But the minstrel merely nodded, took the ring and ran.

Cathbar turned to face the crowd. Fuelled by fear and igno-rance of what was happening, the townspeople were growing restless; there were scuffles with fleeing Guardians, accusa-tions of sorcery flying about.

'HEAR ME!' Cathbar roared.

He smoothed them to silence with a spread of his big arms. 'Your king has spoken. The Guardians are stripped of all authority in the town – and throughout this kingdom.' A ragged cheer broke out, but Cathbar went on. 'I am in com-mand of the king's men-at-arms now, and I tell you this: any man who harms another today, be he Guardian or not, will be hanged! Or woman, too!' he added, glaring out over the crowd. There was a surge of muttering as cobblestones were dropped and men quietly changed their grips on sticks and spades.

'Now,' Cathbar said to the king, 'you have amends to make, my lord. This lad here is indeed Edmund, Heored's son. He and his two companions have done you a great service.'

Beotrich bowed low before Edmund. 'I have done you a grave injustice, my lord. I owe you my hospitality, at least,' he said. 'But what service is this that you have done for us?'

Edmund started to speak, but Cathbar stopped him. 'It concerns Orgrim,' he said shortly. 'I'll have my men bring him to you. Before you see him, there is something I must show you.'

*

When Cathbar and Cluaran were summoned to Beotrich's council room to show the spell book to the thanes, Edmund was left alone with Elspeth in the great hall. Neither of them spoke for a while. She was still pale, and the cuts on her arm looked dark and ugly.

'Elspeth,' Edmund began painfully, 'there's something I must tell you. It's about Orgrim.'

'He's your uncle?'

Edmund was shocked. 'But how did you . . .?'

'He told me,' she said.

'I'm sorry.' It was all Edmund could say.

'What for?' said Elspeth. 'You saved me from him, Edmund! Whatever Orgrim did is nothing to do with you.'

But Edmund still brooded. He and Orgrim had the same gift, and they were kinsmen. Might not the sorcerer's taint have crept inside Edmund like a worm inside an apple? He longed more than ever to go home, to see his mother again. Yet how could he tell her what her beloved brother had become?

Cluaran came back from the Rede Chamber in good spirits. 'We have been pardoned,' he announced. 'Your death warrant has been torn up, Edmund.'

'How did you persuade the thanes that I wasn't a witch?' Elspeth asked, her eyes wide. 'They saw the sword appear in my hand!'

The minstrel's face was guarded. 'The King's Rede of Wessex has its own store of knowledge,' he said carefully. 'Some of the thanes know only too well what the sword is and where it came from. It means that you are an honoured guest here, Elspeth.'

Elspeth looked as if she was mortally uncomfortable at being an honoured guest in a king's house. Edmund changed the subject.

'The thing you said you came to find in Venta,' he said to Cluaran. 'Did you find it?'

Cluaran looked grave. 'Yes, though it was nearly too late. It was stolen from my people some time ago. If Orgrim had possessed the sword as well, no power on earth could have defeated him.'

'What was it?' Edmund asked curiously, wondering if it had been the thing that Cluaran had stowed in his pack before showing them the spell books.

Cluaran shook his head. 'It is not time for you to know. Maybe later, maybe not at all.' He smiled. 'You will be pleased to know that a horseman has already been sent to Dunmonia, to recall Aagard to the court.'

Elspeth's face lit up. 'We'll see him again!' But then she turned to Edmund. 'Or at least we can, if you are able to wait here a few days more? Have you sent word home yet?'

Her concern touched Edmund. 'I'll send a message to my mother tomorrow,' he told her. 'I'll tell her to expect us in a week's time. You will stay with us, won't you, before you go back to Dubris?' As he said this, he recalled what Cluaran had said about the sword, that it would lead Elspeth on a quest whether she wanted it or no. Only Edmund had the choice to go with her, or stay behind with his mother. It felt like an impossible choice to make, and he looked away as he heard her say:

'I'd like that, Edmund. Thank you.'

Beotrich's hospitality was lavish. They ate roast meat with the king's household that night, and Elspeth thought the meal would go on for ever. Afterwards Cluaran was persuaded to play, and the king's face softened as he listened to the lilting music. Elspeth's arm throbbed under the bandage and her whole body ached, but she felt some of her tension lifting. Edmund's offer had been sincerely meant. She'd stay awhile before going back to Dubris, and then to sea again. Yes, back to sea. And why not? Cluaran's talk of evil gods – Loki, the sword – it all seemed like a story now. They had defeated Orgrim and surely that was the end of it.

Elspeth swallowed a yawn, longing for her bed. She was glad when the slaves came to clear the hall. She leaned her elbow on the great oak table, her head resting on her hand, but, over the servants' bustle and hum of conversation, she was gradually aware of a new noise, one she hadn't heard before. It came from outside the great hall – a whirring sound, soft but very deep.

She looked up curiously – and saw Edmund's face rigid with alarm. 'What is it?' she said. But before he could speak, there was a dreadful roar, and the roof of the great hall was peeled off like a man skinning a rabbit.

237

Down swept an icy wind, dousing all the torches. A massive roof beam split and came crashing to the floor. Thanes and slaves alike dived under tables, ran for the doors. Edmund alone stood rooted to the spot, still as stone, his blue eyes wide with horror. Elspeth pushed through the rush of bodies, grabbed his hand and yanked him after her.

'It's come back!' he whispered.

Elspeth dragged him from the hall, close on Cathbar's heels. Outside in the square, the night air was freezing. And yet above them in the sky there was fire, and fire in the streets too. Across the square a grand house roared, its thatch blazing, and Elspeth watched, open-mouthed, as a flame shot over their heads, torching the house next to it. The night swelled to one long, endless scream.

Then Elspeth looked up.

High overhead, where moon and stars should have been, something blocked their light. Huge and dark and terrifying. Another burst of fire scorched the sky, and Elspeth saw the gaping grin, with fangs each taller than a man, and she saw the pearly glimmer of a huge reptilian eye.

Cathbar had seen it too, and barked out orders for bowmen, ropes and torches.

'Torment,' Edmund murmured. 'I felt him coming.'

'But Orgrim has no power now!' Elspeth cried. 'Who is left to summon the dragon?'

Edmund said nothing.

The dragon's eye was clearer now. It rolled towards them as Cathbar's men fired ropes in their bid to drag the monster from the sky. Somewhere in the distance, Elspeth thought she heard Cluaran shout, but she did not move. Beside her, Edmund stared at the sky as if he read his future in the boiling clouds.

The dragon swooped with a thunderous roar. Two taloned feet, vast claws curling, loomed over their heads. Elspeth threw her arms round Edmund and pushed him to the ground. But a long claw brushed them, scythed through the back of Elspeth's woollen gown, and another caught up Edmund's cloak and tunic. Then, its vast wings scraping the housetops, the dragon climbed through the air skywards. Elspeth and Edmund dangled like kittens from its talons.

But the dragon carried someone else out of the square, one man clinging to a rope that had been flung around the monstrous tail. As the dragon started to soar, Captain Cathbar had lashed the other end around his own waist and let himself be carried off into the darkness.

Too late, Cluaran dashed into the square. He cried out after them, 'I should have told you! You've a right to know! Swordbearer, Ripente – what have I condemned you to?'

The minstrel watched in despair as the dragon headed east – a bluish hulk against the black night sky. For a moment it was lit by a flare of white light. Then the light winked out and the dragon was gone.

*

239

Aagard set off for Venta as soon as the horseman brought him the news of Orgrim's fall. He travelled all day and made good progress on the mule. As night fell, and with no cottage near to ask for board and lodging, he found a sheltered ash grove just off the road and set up camp. The night was mild and dry. He'd eaten well on oatcakes and dried herring, was wrapped warmly in his good cloak. But still he could not sleep.

'So they have stopped Orgrim,' he muttered. *By all the stars!* He should be thankful. The sword had fulfilled its destiny. Despite all his fears for the children, and his warnings to them to skirt Venta, the sword had led them there, and between the three of them they had defeated the sorcerer.

It's over.

Turning on his side, Aagard settled down once more and tried to sleep.

Fingers of ice brushed over his cheeks. A snow-wind ripped off his cloak and tossed it away like a leaf.

As he stumbled after it, fear gripped him like a vice. Snow in May? He scanned the sky. Sure enough, far to the East he saw streaks of flame licking the horizon, turning the indigo clouds to scarlet and orange.

Torment the ice dragon was abroad once more.

Aagard picked up his cloak, pulled it round him in the bitter blast.

'No,' he whispered. 'No, it's not over. It has barely begun.'

Read on for a sneak peek at Edmund and
Elspeth's next thrilling adventure in . . .

THE BOOK OF THE SWORD
DARKEST AGE, BOOK TWO

CHAPTER ONE

I knew even then that the fiery light in the north meant war.
But I could not know how much that war would take from me.
[The Book of the Sword]

Elspeth screamed.

A remembered agony shot through her right arm, and with it a sense of overwhelming grief and loss. In the blackness behind her eyelids the vision persisted – the young man kneeling, head bent; the old man staring horrified at his bare hand, both bathed in red light. And the scene stirred memories of her own: of another fire-lit cave; a metal gauntlet found in a sea-wracked chest, and the sword that had sprung so unexpectedly to her own hand. In her strange dream, she knew she had seen the forging of the crystal sword – the blade that was as much a part of her now as her own arm. But who was the young woman – not so much older than Elspeth herself, perhaps – who had played such a willing part in the painful ritual, and had disappeared?

Her arm still throbbed; hurting worse now than it had in the dream. Elspeth suddenly realized that both her arms were pinned painfully to her sides, and she could not feel her legs at all. Was she in prison again? Had the sorcerer Orgrim recaptured her? But surely she and Edmund had escaped, had defeated Orgrim. They had been feasted by the King of Wessex himself . . . hadn't they?

A gust of cold stung her face, and she opened her eyes . . . to find nothing but freezing mist, whipping around her in an unseen wind. She might have been back on her father's ship, carving a path through a winter blizzard – were it not for the way she was gripped, feet dangling, her arms clamped to her body by two great, scaled talons.

Memory scorched back: the dragon! It had ripped the roof off the king's hall; seized her and Edmund . . . Elspeth's heart was suddenly knocking so hard that she could hear it, and there seemed no air to breathe. Biting down on a cry of panic, she peered desperately through the greyness for any sign of Edmund. But there was nothing. The suffocating fog pressed against her on all sides, and she was entirely alone.

No. Never alone.

The voice filled her head and ran through her nerves like lightning. Her arm was throbbing again: looking down, she saw the familiar light of the crystal sword in her right hand, pale and indistinct at first, but growing stronger, more brilliant as she watched.

Beneath her, as if dispelled by the sword's light, the fog had begun to clear. Elspeth could see land far below: an indistinct expanse of white and black glimpsed through swirls of mist. A moment later the last of the mist had gone, replaced by clear blue sky and the dazzling rays of an early-morning sun. The dragon had been flying inside a cloud, Elspeth realized. Below her now was a landscape of ice and snow, barred with soft light. To one side lay a swathe of stippled darkness that might be a forest; to the other, the sun was just showing its face between mountains white with snow, their tops pink-lit by the dawn sky.

I am with you until our task is done.

What task? Elspeth wondered. What was she expected to do, in this alien land? Did the sword have some plan for her, even now? The blade's glow in her hand seemed to pulse, like the heartbeat of a living thing, and a sudden suspicion seized her: *the sword wanted me here.*

What are you doing to me? she demanded. *Did you bring me here?*

The voice in her head was silent. *Answer me!* she insisted.

This is where we must be, the voice said at last. *But not like this – not in the dragon's claws.* And a sudden terror filled her: the sword's fear that, after all, the great plan would fail

– if Elspeth could not free herself.

'*What* plan?' In her exasperation, Elspeth had spoken aloud, but the wind whipped her words away before her ears could hear them. At that moment the beast holding her banked, tilting her sickeningly sideways as it veered towards the mountains, and she saw Edmund.

He was hanging limply from the dragon's other front claw, too far away to call to, even without the whistling wind in her ears. From this angle she could see little but his white-blond hair and the once-fine blue cloak, now hanging around him in tatters. His head hung down as if he were unconscious, and what she could see of his face was as pale as his linen shirt.

There was a flicker of movement in the air above him, and Elspeth's gaze flashed in alarm to the great blue-scaled foreleg that held him. It was as thick around as an oak, double-jointed like a lizard's and folded back against the great barred underbelly that filled the sky above her. The sheer size of the creature that held them made her shudder afresh, but there *was* something moving there, something small and fast, even higher up. She twisted her neck painfully, scanning up and along the blue-black mass to where it joined the body . . . There. A tiny brown figure was clinging to the dragon's shoulder. No, not tiny: a grown

man, with a rope around his waist and a sword in his belt –
who looked down and jerked his head in greeting.

Cathbar!

She had no time to wonder how the captain came to be
there. He had passed his rope right around the dragon's
great forelimb: his perch was precarious, but he had both
arms free as he signalled her. He pointed to the snowy
ground far below, making opening and closing gestures
with one hand. Then he drew his sword.

Elspeth understood him at once, and her first response
was *No!* He could not attack the dragon in flight! The fall
would kill them, all three. But Cathbar was gesturing again,
his face impatient. She looked down again. They were
much closer to the ground than before. The black clumps
below were recognizable as trees: she could even see the
snow on their top branches. But Edmund still dangled unconscious from the dragon's claw – how could he survive?

Cathbar pointed again, straight ahead this time. She followed his gesture – and suddenly understood. They were
heading for the mountains. Jagged cliffs of grey stone
loomed ahead of them: there would be no surviving *that*
fall. And if they did not fight – if the dragon were allowed
to take them to its master . . . She forced her gaze back to
Cathbar, and nodded once.

Smoothly, without a moment's wait, the man swung himself into the hollow of the dragon's shoulder and stabbed upwards. The first stroke brought barely a shudder to the claw holding Elspeth, but a low rumbling began to shake the air around her. At the second stroke a great convulsion whipped Elspeth through the air like a fish on a line. White earth and blue air whirled around her while above the great throat pulsed with an agonized roar. Out of the corner of one eye she saw a tree-like limb flailing through the air; saw Edmund, released, drop like a wounded bird.

She had time to breathe a few words of a prayer for Edmund's life before another convulsion shook her. Bucking and plunging in the air, she saw the fight in flashes: a gout of black blood oozing from the dragon's chest; Cathbar, the rope only holding his feet, leaning dangerously far over the beast's shoulder as he tried to strike closer to the throat. Then the great head swung round, cutting off her view.

For an instant, as the dragon tried to reach its own chest, Elspeth caught sight of its cavernous mouth; the smoking pit of a nostril, and then the huge eye filled her sight. She could swear the eye focused on her, filled with a cold and terrifying hatred: *you won't escape me!*

'Sword!' she whispered desperately, and the sword

seemed to writhe in her hand, pulsing in rhythm with her own blood. But she could not move her arm to lift it. The claw gripping her was clenched so tightly that she could hardly breathe.

The dragon had found the source of its pain. The great head snaked upward, sending a jet of blue flame along its shoulder. Cathbar hurled himself out of the way, his clothes burning; the scorched end of the rope whipped through the air as the dragon drew its head back to swat him into the sky. Before her vision was cut off Elspeth caught one last glimpse of him, lunging forward for a final blow.

The dragon screamed – and the talon gripping Elspeth slackened its grasp. Her arm was so numb she hardly knew how she moved it, but she managed a wild swipe at the limb above her head. Below her she saw Cathbar falling, a trail of blue fire following him like the tail of a comet. And then she was plunging after him, rolling over and over in the air, the sword flashing and the wind whistling about her, until the world went white.

A. J. LAKE is a former teacher with a lifelong interest in the period of British history known as the Dark Ages. She is inspired by mountians, storms and places of ice and snow. And she secretly hopes that dragons are real.

www.thedarkestage.com